W9-AFL-352

"You'll never make a go of it," Alex said

"You don't know that," Carla challenged. "I'm a Hepburn as well, you know." She could sense the same deep-running passion for possession in Alex that stirred in herself, and it brought with it a strange and exhilarating excitement.

But it was completely unexpected when her arms were gripped by hard strong fingers suddenly, and she was swung around. Alex's face loomed above her.

"Green eyes!" Alex declared in a thick, rough voice that breathed warm against her lips. "Green-eyed women are aye stubborn, but there's ways of taming stubborn creatures like you, Carla girl."

She struggled in his hold, but his mouth was already on hers, fierce and hard; then with a laugh he released her and went striding off down the path.

OTHER
Harlequin Romances
by LUCY GILLEN

Many of these titles are available at your local bookseller.

For a free catalogue listing all available Harlequin Romances,
send your name and address to:

HARLEQUIN READER SERVICE,
M.P.O. Box 707, Niagara Falls, N.Y. 14302
Canadian address: Stratford, Ontario, Canada N5A 6W2

Hepburn's Quay

by

LUCY GILLEN

Harlequin Books

TORONTO • LONDON • NEW YORK • AMSTERDAM
SYDNEY • HAMBURG • PARIS • STOCKHOLM

Original hardcover edition published in 1979
by Mills & Boon Limited

ISBN 0-373-02319-7

Harlequin edition published March 1980

Copyright © 1979 by Lucy Gillen.
Philippine copyright 1979. Australian copyright 1979.

All rights reserved. Except for use in any review, the reproduction or utilization
of this work in whole or in part in any form by any electronic, mechanical or
other means, now known or hereafter invented, including xerography,
photocopying and recording, or in any information storage or retrieval system,
is forbidden without the permission of the publisher. All the characters in this
book have no existence outside the imagination of the author and have no
relation whatsoever to anyone bearing the same name or names. They are not
even distantly inspired by any individual known or unknown to the author, and
all the incidents are pure invention.

The Harlequin trademark, consisting of the word HARLEQUIN and the
portrayal of a Harlequin, is registered in the United States Patent Office and
the Canada Trade Marks Office.

Printed in U.S.A.

CHAPTER ONE

THE main road had been left behind them some time
ago, and they were now travelling along a narrow by-
way that dipped and curved with the tortuousness of a
switchback, offering fresh vistas at every turn. To Carla
the journey was a familiar one, for she had done it so
many times before, and she watched eagerly for land-
marks, refreshing her memory each time some particular aspect struck a chord. It was more than a year since
she came last, but nothing was forgotten, only tucked
away at the back of her mind and easily recalled.

But to Tom Laxey at the wheel of the car it was
completely new terrain, and he clucked and cursed in
exasperation as he coped with the constantly changing
direction and the repeated ups and downs which
allowed little time for sightseeing. He had not even
found time to say very much either, apart from a series
of irate opinions on the nature of the terrain.

In fact there was little to find fault with. Misty blue
hills beckoned them on, and seemed always to be
further away than they looked, dancing like a lure before them. The steep slopes bristling with dark woods
and sweeping dark shadows of greyish-green heather
that plunged downward to a vast mirror of placid
water, its surface unruffled by a light wind because of
the sheltering hills.

The road was slashed across the face of other hills
and followed the same route as a single railway track
that snaked along above the trees, clinging precariously
between long granite tunnels. Huge cliffs frowned
down at them from one side of the road, with clumps
of pale primrose-green nestling in the crevices, along

with lichen, and summer-green trees that thrived at breathtaking angles above their heads.

On the other side the granite was cut away suddenly as if by a huge knife, and ragged shelves of fir, goat-willow and rowan marched confidently down to the still waters of the loch. It had been raining some time before and the vari-coloured green leaves glistened and gleamed in the pale sunshine, while fat white cumulus clouds ambled across a light blue sky like contented sheep.

It was all just as beautiful as Carla remembered it, and she smiled to herself as they swept downward yet again, only to start climbing again almost at once. She gave all her attention to the scenery for the moment and almost forgot the presence of her companion, even though she had been listening to his complaints for the last mile or two with more amusement than sympathy.

It was only when he addressed her directly, breaking into his flow of increasingly virulent language to do so, that she gave him her attention. 'Are you *sure* this is the only way to get there?' he asked. 'I can't believe that anybody voluntarily comes all the way out here to live. We haven't seen a house for at least four miles— probably five, and we've passed only one car.'

'Two cars and a cattle truck, actually,' Carla corrected him, and laughed.

'It isn't civilised,' he complained. 'The road is diabolical! It's like driving a dodgem car on a switchback circuit!'

'Poor Tom!' Carla gave him her attention for a moment, patting his arm consolingly as he hastily coped with a two-in-one incline that threatened to stand the car on end. 'Never mind, it isn't much further now. There should be a turning just down here on the left past those trees, that takes you direct to Hepburn's Quay.'

Tom took a chance on sending them hurtling off the road at the next bend, and turned his head briefly to look at her. 'You mean we're nearly there?'

'Just down here and on the left,' Carla promised. 'It leads us right to the house.'

'A private road?'

He looked as if he liked the idea of that, but Carla's slight grimace denied the exclusive use of the road in question, although apart from traffic to and from the Carse, it was a private road, she supposed. She did not yet tell him that it was in fact little more than a track that always became deeply rutted in the winter rains and dried into deep troughs in summer—conditions that made for a very bumpy ride indeed. Time enough to discover that for himself.

'It's not exactly exclusive to Hepburn's Quay,' she demured. 'But it does give us access.'

'Well, thank heaven for that anyway!' said Tom with such fervour that she looked at him a little dubiously.

'You're not very impressed with Scotland so far, are you, Tom?'

He gave her a brief rueful grin over his shoulder and changed gear swiftly at the same time. 'I feel a bit like an alien,' he confessed. 'I've been all over Europe at various times, but I've never been further north than Stratford-on-Avon, and I keep expecting some of your fierce forebears to spring out from among the heather and cut my throat with their dirks, or whatever.'

Carla laughed. 'You idiot!' she chided him. 'Anyway, this is Hepburn country and you're with a Hepburn, you won't come to any harm.'

He took another turn, hair-raising on the steep downward slope, and slowed almost to a standstill while he negotiated it. 'No, frankly, darling, I was quite impressed until we started on this road and ever

since, when I've had time to think between praying
for our survival, I can't imagine how the Scots got their
reputation for being the world's best engineers, when
they created a monster like this particular stretch.'

Quite confident and not in the least anxious about
his response, Carla smiled. 'It takes a lot of concentra-
tion, doesn't it?' she said cheerfully. 'I used to love it
when we came up to see Grampy and Grandma when
I was a child. I thought all this up and down business
was great fun.'

Tom cast her a brief rueful glance. 'I can believe it,'
he said. 'But then you weren't driving, were you? It's
enough to—— Hey! Is *that* our turning?'

He applied the brakes and pointed through the
windscreen at a large white board printed in black.
HEPBURN'S CARSE, it read, in letters too big for
anyone to miss, but Carla was frowning curiously.
What she remembered was a ragged grass bank with
the rough spiky grass straggling down over the deeply
rutted track, but instead the corner was neatly shaped
and curved and led smoothly on to a well-surfaced road
that was much wider than the track she remembered.

Tom had brought the car to a halt just short of the
turning, and he was sitting there patiently, waiting for
Carla to confirm the fact that this was indeed their
turning. She looked back up the hill and then ahead at
the winding ribbon of road that curved out of sight
around yet another corner, and she shrugged her
shoulders.

'It must be the turning,' she said. 'Although it didn't
look anything like this the last time I saw it.'

She hadn't noticed as they came down the hill, but
the grassland bordering the road was not open to the
road as it had always been before, but firmly fenced in,
and in the distance, near the loch, a huge herd of red
and white cattle grazed quietly in the sun. The whole

outlook had a neat and orderly appearance that was quite different from what she remembered, and yet it was quite definitely the same place. She gazed at it a moment longer, feeling oddly cheated because everything was not exactly as it had always been, then she shrugged again.

'But this is the turning, Tom, I know it is.'

Studiously patient, Tom looked to her for guidance before he made a move. 'Do we turn down here, then?'

Carla nodded, strangely uneasy suddenly. 'Yes; I don't know of any other way in.'

Putting the car into motion again, Tom once more consulted the big notice board as they drove past it. 'It says Hepburn's Carse, not Hepburn's Quay,' he pointed out.

'Yes, that's right; the road leads to the Quay and to the Carse.' She anticipated his question and went on, 'Hepburn's Carse is the valley, the open land between the hills where the river runs, but it's the name of a house as well. It's just around the other end of the loch. It must have been Alex who put that notice up.'

'Ah!' He sounded as if he understood, although Carla doubted if he really did. She did not quite understand it herself, although if Alex was back there were bound to be changes, she supposed. 'What's that ahead? Do we go straight on, or turn?' Tom broke into her musing and she answered quickly and a little breathlessly, her heart banging hard in her breast suddenly when she saw the old house straight ahead of them.

'Straight on,' she said. 'That's Hepburn's Quay!'

Whether or not Tom was affected by the sight of their goal, there was no doubt about Carla's own reaction; it was just as it had always been. There was always something very special about the first sight of the old house, and she thanked heaven that it at least showed no sign of being other than it had always been.

Carla had been born at Hepburn's Quay, twenty-three years before, but her father's work had taken the young family to the south of England before she was two years old. Since then they had come back each summer for as long as her mother was alive; less often after she died. It had been her mother's home and Charles Francis had had no heart for visiting it when he lost his wife, although Carla had been once or twice on her own. The last time had been just over a year ago; the last time she had seen Grampy Hepburn.

It was her grandfather, Fergus Hepburn, who had willed Hepburn's Quay to her when he died nearly six months ago. And Carla never ceased to regret that she had been unable to come and pay him her last respects with the rest of the Hepburns, because she was laid low with an attack of influenza. She had not known her Grandmother Hepburn so well because she died when Carla was quite small, but she had loved Grampy very much.

It was that fact made this particular arrival all the more bitter-sweet somehow, and she felt a momentary prickle of tears as Tom drove the car along the brand new road to where Hepburn's Quay stood at the loch-side, mellow and serene as always. Just as she remembered it from all those other times.

The new road came to an abrupt end at the same tumbledown gate she remembered; Grampy never had got around to mending it, and it seemed not to matter that it had been pressed back into the thick thorn hedge for so long that it had become almost a part of it. The garden looked neglected, as it had never been in her grandfather's time, and it gave an additional air of sadness to the old place that was alarmingly affecting.

'Well——' Tom opened the car door for her and she stepped out on to the springy dark turf, sniffing the familiar scents of gorse and peaty brown water, while clean fresh air stirred her reddish-brown hair and freshened her skin. 'We arrived, anyway.'

Carla stood beside him and her green eyes had a soft, absent look as she recalled all the other times she had stood at the edge of the loch and gazed across at the hills that crowded in on every side, making the carse mild and sheltered even in winter. She remembered the tranquillity of silence, although it was now filled with the low muffled lowing of the cattle across on the other side of the loch.

'It's beautiful,' she said in a voice that was not quite steady. 'I always loved it here.'

She knew the big old house was going to remind her of Grampy, and that she was going to miss him; it couldn't be the same without him. But it was all new to Tom, and she must try to see it from his point of view, try to give him the same feel for the old place that she had herself, if it was possible.

A glance at his face suggested that he was less impressed than she hoped, but then Tom Laxey was a town man and made no pretence of being anything other. The wonder was that he had decided to come all this way to somewhere as isolated as Hepburn's Quay, even for the sake of a business venture. He was a shrewd business man, just as his father was, and Carla had worked as his secretary for more than a year, but when he had suggested going into partnership with her, it had come as a surprise.

At the back of her mind she knew that a business partnership was not the only thing Tom had in mind, but he had shown sufficient enthusiasm for her idea of turning her inheritance into an hotel, and she had preferred to see it as his only interest. There was a little money from her grandfather's estate too, but not nearly enough to make full-scale alterations, and if Tom was sufficiently taken with Hepburn's Quay to help finance the scheme, then she was agreeable to the business side of the association anyway. Although she had not so far committed herself wholeheartedly, it was to discover whether or not the plan was practicable that she and Tom had driven up from London.

'What do you think, Tom?'

She looked at him fairly confidently, for although she knew he was not a countryman at heart, not even the most unappreciative man could remain unmoved by such surroundings. But he did not look at the scene before them, as Carla did, he turned instead to look at the house, and shrugged, making a grimace with his mouth at the same time.

'Let's go and take a look inside before I commit myself too far,' he suggested. 'It certainly looks solid enough from outside.'

A little disappointed, Carla nodded, once more experiencing that same sense of loss when she faced the house, because she anticipated how empty it would be without Grampy. 'I meant the view,' she said while they walked into the garden, past the tumbledown gate and up to the front door by way of a wide, unweeded path. 'Don't you think it's worth anyone's time and trouble to drive here just for that view, Tom?'

'I'm sure of it, darling,' Tom agreed, with a smile that made allowances for nostalgia, and which Carla found vaguely irritating. 'But paying guests, the sort we have in mind, would expect a hell of a lot more than a view for their money, you know. They'll expect central heating, bathrooms, Cordon Bleu cooking, the lot. Did your granddad have electricity and main drainage? Piped water and sound floorboards, without dry rot?'

'Oh, Tom, I don't know!' Carla felt he was going too fast, and yet she had to allow that there were a great many things that would have to be considered if they were to make Hepburn's Quay into a good class hotel. 'There's electricity and water, I know, and there's a bathroom, but the rest—well, I simply don't know. They aren't the kind of things you think about when you stay with family. I always loved it here and I didn't look for drawbacks.'

Tom's arm slid around her waist while she took the key from her handbag and pushed it into the keyhole with a slightly unsteady hand. 'No, of course you didn't, love.' He kissed her cheek, lightly and confidently, then ushered her in through the door in front of him. 'But they're the kind of things that have to be taken into account when you're offering a service to paying customers. I'm just looking at the project practically, that's all, I'm not running down your inheritance.'

It was a curious feeling to come into the wide hall and not see the familiar grey-haired figure, standing with open arms and a broad smile, waiting for her, and Carla swallowed hard. It looked very much the same, except that there was an air about it that it had never had when the house was lived in. An air of flat emptiness that brought a slight shiver to her skin and made Tom slip his arm through hers, drawing her close to his side for a moment.

Otherwise it was the same. The polished wood-block floor, bloomed over now with neglect, and the rich Indian rugs that had been her grandmother's pride and joy, dulled slightly with a patina of dust. Sentimental Victorian pictures in heavy gilt frames, sharing the slightly grubby walls with one or two better paintings, and the wide staircase that rose from almost the exact centre of the hall.

There was a smell too; the smell of neglect, of dampness perhaps, and it reminded her of what Tom had said about dry rot. But for the moment she could not face finding fault with anything, and for the first time since they set out, she wished she could have seen the old house again when she was alone. Tom would not see it as she did, nor appreciate the memories it brought back, and she turned to look at him after a moment or two, to try and judge what his first impression was, hoping the slight mistiness in her eyes was apparent only to herself.

'Well?' she asked, a little breathlessly.

Tom's good-looking features were carefully controlled. Perhaps he was more sensitive to her feelings than she realised, or perhaps he was quite genuinely pleased with the old-fashioned comfort it suggested, even in its present state of neglect. 'Quite impressive,' he said. 'But shall we do a complete tour of inspection before I make any observations?'

Carla nodded. He was being kind for her sake, she felt quite sure now, but it made her feel strangely out of touch with him suddenly, as she never had been before. Hepburn's Quay meant so much more to her than it did to Tom, and for quite different reasons, but she had to try and keep her mind on the same practical plane as his if their partnership was going to work.

The house *was* old-fashioned, and the more she saw of it, the more Carla was forced to recognise just how much needed to be done to turn it into even a run-of-the-mill hotel, let alone the kind of place that Tom had in mind. There were eight bedrooms, only four of which were furnished, and only one that had been regularly used, by her grandfather. There were two bathrooms, but only one was really usable and neither had a modern hot-water system, although all the years she had stayed there Carla had never realised the second bathroom lacked any means of heating water.

Hepburn's Quay had been a solitary home for one old man for far too long and it seemed nothing like it had when Carla stayed there last, only a year earlier.

Because, she realised as they walked along the silent and gloomy landing, she was seeing it through different eyes this time.

As she followed Tom up another and narrower flight of stairs to the attic rooms, she wondered if she had not been far too optimistic with her plans. But then her somewhat jaundiced pessimism received a nudge when she gazed out of one of the windows at the view. It was possible to see for miles, even allowing for the restriction of those hazy blue hills that were never as close as they seemed to be.

The carse stretched out around and beyond its own small loch, and a river flowed through like a silver-grey ribbon that curved suddenly to skirt around the loch, trapping a long strip of solid ground between the two of them before swerving off again towards the hills, snaking across the carse into the distance.

It was only now that Carla noticed how that strip of solid ground too had been converted to a properly surfaced road as it curved around towards the big house at the far end of the loch. Alex again, she guessed, and watched, suddenly alert, when a long black car came skimming into view and went speeding along the road towards Hepburn's Carse. It might not be Alex, but even the possibility of it being him brought a stirring of that special kind of excitement that she had not experienced for more than six years, and which she now hastily stifled, turning her head to take in other aspects instead.

A new white ranch-type fence neatly enclosed a section of pasture up nearer the house, and she attributed that to Alex too, for it was not the kind of venture she could imagine old Annie taking any interest in. Seeing it there, so bold and newly neat among the softer and more familiar features of Hepburn's Carse, she felt a curious sense of resentment, although it would have been stupid to expect everything to be exactly the same with Alex back. New ideas, new prospects for the old place, that had been his aim when he went for those five years to Canada, and that starkly new fencing was one of them, no doubt.

Tom's hand touching lightly on her shoulder made her turn from the window with a strange unrest in her heart, and from the corner of her eye she could still see the speeding car making its way around the loch, distracting her. So she turned right around so that it was cut from her field of view, facing Tom but smiling as she looked up at him; excluding him from her private thoughts because he would never understand them.

'These attic rooms have the best view of all, I think,' she ventured. 'They're quite a decent size too.'

Tom glanced around at the low-ceilinged room with sunlight dappling the faded walls and showing up the dust of neglect, emphasising the shabbiness, drawing out the damp, fusty smell of disuse. 'They're certainly big enough,' he agreed, and Carla once again sensed his caution; that undisguised reluctance to become caught up in her enthusiasm.

'I thought,' Carla pressed on, refusing to be discouraged, 'they'd be ideal for living quarters. There are three of them, and that would leave a spare one for a—a housekeeper, someone like that. Of course I know you'd have to go back, you'll be needed in London, but I could have a permanent place here and you could come whenever you——'

'I should have to stay and keep an eye on my investment,' Tom interrupted quietly. 'I couldn't leave it all to you, could I?'

He slipped an arm around her waist and drew her towards him, seemingly unaware that she had stiffened slightly, and managed somehow to keep a certain distance between them still. His blue eyes were warm and smiling and had a look in them that Carla recognised and rather regretted at this particular moment.

'If you married me,' he whispered with his lips brushing her forehead while he spoke, 'we could not only save a room but make way for extra staff or even another guest.'

Whatever Carla had been expecting it was not this rather roundabout proposal, and she wondered if he was entirely serious about it. She had been out with him quite often when they were in London and she worked for his father's firm, but she had been with other men-friends as well, so he could not claim her exclusive company had given him the idea. Whatever was behind it, she wished he had not chosen this moment to make the gesture, not when she was trying to come to terms with what she should do with Hepburn's Quay.

Deciding to pass it off as merely a lighthearted gesture, she smiled and moved easily out of his embrace, pacing the long empty room as she spoke. 'I'm flattered, Tom,' she told him as if she did not for a moment believe he was serious, 'but this is strictly a business partnership, remember? Shall we go and look at the loch again, and the quay? It would be an added attraction, don't you think, if we could have boats on the loch?'

He was wearing a slight frown when she glanced at him, and a rather sheepish expression, so that she feared he might have been serious, or at least half serious, after all, and she felt sorry about it. In that mood, she took his hand when he came and joined her in the doorway and they went downstairs and outside again, in more or less total silence.

Outside in the warm, soft sunshine, the air smelled a great deal fresher than the mustiness of the old house, and they made for the quay so that Tom could judge for himself what an asset it would be. The garden hedge was straggly and untrimmed and it petered out some five or six feet from the edge of the small granite quay that gave the place its name.

It was only about ten or eleven feet wide and built of flat grey granite slabs that were worn down with age to a smooth, almost polished surface. There was a mooring ring at one end, but no boat now, and a wooden post that leaned so far outwards that the wonder was it did not fall into the loch. Like everything else, it looked so much more neglected than Carla remembered it, and gave her a sense of sadness.

'It has possibilities,' Tom conceded, but with the same caution he had displayed about everything so far. Pointing across to where the river glinted greyly in the sun as it curved around the loch for some distance before heading off for the hills, he frowned curiously. 'Is that ours, that river?'

His use of the possessive 'ours' was a form of encouragement, Carla supposed as she followed his direction, and she wondered if he realised how little of the surrounding land actually belonged to her grandfather's estate. 'Not the river,' she told him. 'That's on the carse and belongs to them. It sometimes floods in winter, but it doesn't affect this house as a rule, only the Carse, being on lower ground.'

She indicated the house at the end of the loch and Tom looked at it with narrowed eyes. 'Any relation?' he asked, referring to the name. 'Hepburn's Carse—I wondered if it was the same clan.'

'They're related, but not closely,' Carla agreed. 'Old Annie Hepburn lives there still, and Alex, of course.'

'Alex?' He asked the question casually and with apparently little interest, but Carla knew him well enough now, to know just how deceptive that was. 'You mentioned him as being responsible for putting up that notice board at the end of the road,' he reminded her.

It was startling how easy it was to remember her old feeling for Alex, and she shrugged uneasily, answering with a carelessness she hoped was not too obviously assumed. 'I suppose he's a cousin, but I haven't seen him for years. He's old Annie's grandson and he's lived here with her for most of his life, except for the five years he spent in Canada. He's back now, and Grampy told me he's running the estate like a Wild West cattle ranch.' She sensed he was interested and was nothing loath to enlighten him further. 'My mother and Alex's father were second cousins, although they're both gone now, of course, like Grampy.'

'But auld Annie still marches on, och aye!'

His slightly mocking attempt at a Scottish accent brought only a faint smile from her, for her own grandfather had been very definitely Scottish in his speech, and she loved to hear it. 'She's about ninety-two, I think. She married one of old Johnnie Hepburn's grandsons; she actually remembers him, in fact.'

'Local character?' Tom suggested, and Carla laughed, pulling a face when she admitted to her notorious ancestor.

'Johnnie Hepburn had a reputation, in inverted commas,' she told him, 'and he lived to be over ninety. He had fourteen legitimate children and heaven knows how many others, but only two of his sons survived to marry and have families of their own—my great-grandfather and Alex's. Alex's had ten children, all respectable, and it was *his* eldest son that old Annie married.'

'Holy smoke!' Tom whistled through his teeth. 'They're a—prolific lot, the Hepburns, aren't they? I don't think I'd fancy trying to feed and clothe a regiment like that on today's prices!' He slid a hand beneath her arm and squeezed lightly, smiling down at her with eyes that glinted warmly. 'Not that I've anything against a family,' he added. 'All in good time.'

Avoiding any chance of a more intimate situation, Carla brought him firmly back to present matters, although she had to admit that she was not altogether averse to the idea of Tom as a husband—some time in the future though, not now. 'The most pressing question is how to go about feeding and housing our guests,' she reminded him. 'Always providing this scheme comes off and you really think it's a viable proposition. Do you, Tom?'

He did not look at her and Carla wished he would, because she felt he was thinking things he did not want her to know, when he avoided her eyes like that. But whatever opinion he would have expressed, she was not destined to hear it at the moment, for something else had taken his eye and she followed his gaze curiously when he nodded his head.

A horseman was coming towards them across the carse, skirting the loch and taking the short way round, riding easily, not hurrying but still obviously coming to join them. And Carla's heart gave a breathtaking lurch that almost choked her when she realised who he was. It was six years since she last saw Alex Hepburn, and he had changed. Not obviously, but in various subtle ways that it was not even possible to spot at first.

Not that he had grown from boy to man in that time, for he had already been a widower of twenty-nine with a young son, when he left for Canada. But he had grown more hard-looking and his strong, rugged face looked even more dour than she remembered it. A deep, remote man, who rode as he had always done, with confidence and a certain air of arrogance that sat well on him. But he was thirty-five years old, and whatever boyishness he had possessed had yielded completely to a mature and rugged masculinity.

Long legs in fawn cord trousers straddled the broad back of a grey stallion whose wilful head he held firmly with strong brown hands, and a fawn shirt opened at the neck to show a muscular throat and a vee of tanned skin. His hair was thick, the same red-brown colour as her own, the colour of the Hepburns, and his mouth had a firm straightness that relaxed only a little when he reined in his mount and slid down to stand facing them.

The brown eyes were something that Carla remembered well, and she tried hard to forget that at seventeen she had thought Alex Hepburn the sexiest and most attractive man she had ever seen, even though he was more than twelve years her senior and hardly the kind of smooth charmer that young girls are prone to adore. He had, she remembered ruefully, never given her the slightest encouragement, and yet she had dreamed of him long after he went to Canada, and even wept on occasion because she feared she might never see him again.

'Carla?' The brown eyes questioned her so much more gently than the rather brusque voice, and she nodded.

'That's right, Alex. Have I changed so much that you weren't sure?'

'You've grown up.' The answer was brief and to the point, and she wondered why she coloured so furiously. It was maddening to think he could still make her blush like a schoolgirl just by looking at her. 'I'm very sorry about Uncle Fergus—your grandfather. I was very fond of him.'

The confession was somehow very touching and a lump rose once more in her throat, making it hard to swallow. He had so far concentrated solely on her, but he looked at Tom suddenly with the obvious intention of discovering who he was, so that Carla hastily effected an introduction.

'Oh, this is Tom Laxey, a friend of mine. Tom, this is Alex Hepburn. I suppose you're a distant cousin, aren't you, Alex?'

The two men shook hands, but it startled Carla to detect a definite air of suspicion between them. They eyed each other with undisguised wariness, and she was at a loss to understand why, though Alex was quite plainly curious to know where Tom fitted into the scheme of things.

'The relationship's too distant to claim we're cousins, I would say,' Alex declared unhesitatingly, and Carla detected just a hint of trans-Atlantic twang in the deep Scottish voice.

'How's Colin?'

Alex did not quite frown, it was only a slight drawing of his reddish brows, but he did not look directly at her when he answered. 'He's well, thank you,' he told her. 'And Grandmother wishes to be remembered to you.'

'Did she know I was coming?'

Carla smiled at the idea, for there was little that old Annie Hepburn did not know about, she had a reputation for it. Although heaven alone knew where she got most of her information from. And when Alex looked at her, just briefly, his brown eyes were warmed by a suggestion of a smile, for he was as familiar as anyone else with his grandmother's infallible nose for news.

'Oh aye,' he said quietly, 'she knew.'

'She's wonderful,' Carla enthused with genuine affection for the old lady. 'It was just over a year ago when I saw her last, and I thought she was incredible for her age.'

Alex nodded, but his eyes were watching her closely,

seeking more information, and not above asking for
confirmation of what he had heard rumoured. 'She's
also heard that you're thinking of living here at the
Quay,' he said. 'Is that right, Carla?'

After only a brief glance at Tom, Carla nodded. 'I'm
not just thinking about it,' she told him. 'I'm definitely
staying here.'

'I see.'

His lack of enthusiasm was hardly encouraging, and
Carla felt a curious niggling of disappointment that he
did not immediately welcome the idea of her as a
permanent neighbour. But if he had exclaimed smil-
ingly and enthusiastically over the prospect he would
not have been the Alex she remembered. And no matter how much older they had both grown in the past
six years, she still found the quiet, virile version of
Alex Hepburn dangerously attractive.

'I've some business I'd like to discuss with you some
time,' he told her, but made no attempt to enlighten
her further.

Instead he turned and remounted, while Carla
frowned curiously at his broad back. Seated on the
huge grey horse once more, he towered over them,
which seemed somehow to add to the air of remoteness
about him, and Carla's smile trembled uncertainly in
the face of it. 'What can you possibly have to discuss
with me in the way of business?' she asked. 'What's it
about, Alex?'

He held the animal's wilful head firmly and turned
him round so that it was possible for him to look down
at her directly, flicking a brief but telling glance in
Tom's direction before he spoke. 'It's a private matter,'
he said. 'I'll call around and see you some time when
it's more convenient. 'Bye, Carla—Mr Laxey.'

It was so obvious that he wanted to see her without
Tom being there that Tom flushed to the roots of his

hair with indignation, and only Carla's hand on his arm prevented him from telling about their proposed partnership. Whether Alex noticed or not, she had no idea, but he briefly raised one hand in a half-salute, then jabbed his heels into the horse's flanks and set off back the way he had come.

Watching him go, Tom glared after his retreating back. 'Surly devil!' he declared shortly. 'Sorry if he's one of your clan, darling, but he isn't my cup of tea! He very obviously didn't like me being here, and I don't like being looked at down his autocratic Scottish nose as if I was one of the peasants!' He glared again after Alex's retreating figure. 'Arrogant devil!'

Unwilling to add to his injured feelings by defending Alex, Carla too watched the tall confident figure riding back to Hepburn's Carse. But it was not anger and resentment that she felt, only a strange sense of anticipation. Alex Hepburn *was* arrogant, and he was proud, but one thing she was certain of—after six years he was just as stunningly virile and masculine, and even more unattainable.

CHAPTER TWO

IT was not the most comfortable way to spend a night, in a sleeping bag on top of one of the beds, but Carla had slept well for all that, and woke feeling a tingle of excitement. It was something she could not understand, until she roused herself further and remembered that she had taken possession of Hepburn's Quay, and all the plans she had for it.

From the amount of grumbling he did first thing, it might have been supposed that Tom had fared less well, but Carla suspected that his complaints were made more on principle than from lack of sleep. Tom was not used to roughing it, and until they could organise something more comfortable, they would be living rather rough; at least compared with what he was accustomed to.

He sat watching her make breakfast and did not even offer to make the coffee, which she gathered was likely to be the way of things. Tom was not accustomed to fending for himself either, although Carla vowed she would do something about it before very long. There was something disturbingly intimate about the present situation, she realised as she carefully speared a slice of bread on to the end of an old-fashioned toasting fork. They were virtually living together, even though they were not sharing a bed, and it was not something she had given much thought to until now.

As he looked up suddenly and caught her eye, it seemed Tom must have sensed something of what was going through her mind, for he reached out for one of her hands and squeezed her fingers lightly. 'I like this idea,' he said, his blue eyes gleaming. 'It's very cosy, isn't it? Do you know, Carla darling, I could quite happily go on sitting here all day, gazing into your lovely green eyes.'

Pulling free, Carla thrust the toasting fork into his hand instead, and positioned it in front of the fire-grid. 'You'll be much more gainfully employed making the toast while I cook the rest of our breakfast,' she told him, only slightly breathless. 'And try not to burn it, please, Tom.'

'You're a hard woman!' he declared, but he nevertheless obediently held the bread in front of the fire. He was not happy about being rebuffed, Carla knew, and he watched her from the corners of his eyes while she gingerly removed the cover from the hob of the old-fashioned kitchen range, and stood a frying pan over the glowing fire. 'You just wait!' he murmured ominously.

Carla said nothing. Getting involved seriously with Tom was not her first priority at the moment, and she was doing her best to avoid it, so that she turned quickly and with inward relief when she heard footsteps coming along the garden path. It was difficult to identify the caller at first glance, through the kitchen window and across the width of the room. But then the tall, thin figure came closer and the features below the shock of reddish-brown hair grew more distinct, and she quickly pulled back the frying pan from the hob, leaving the glowing red hole open while she hurried across to greet the newcomer.

'Colin! How are you? Come in!'

She was at the door long before he could knock, smiling a welcome and drawing him into the big warm kitchen with her. The boy smiled, a shy reluctant smile that slowly warmed his grey eyes, and he held out a hand in a touchingly formal gesture, while his gaze darted more warily in Tom's direction.

It was hard to believe that Colin was only eight years younger than she was, for he was still very much a schoolboy at fifteen. Carla had always felt vaguely sorry for him, although on the face of it there was little enough reason for it; for although he had lost his mother at birth, and had been deprived of his father for five years, old Annie doted on her great-grandson as much as any mother could have done on an only child. But there was an air of wistfulness about the boy always, which was something he had more likely inherited from his mother than from his more forceful Hepburn relations.

He was tall like his father, but thin as yet rather than lean and muscular, and he did not have Alex's brown eyes, but the cool, grey and rather shy ones of the mother he had never known. Putting down the carrier bag he carried on the kitchen table, he stepped back as if he was prepared to leave again immediately.

'Aren't you going to sit down for a few minutes before you go back?' Carla urged, but he shook his head.

'I only came to bring the oatcakes and butter from the farm,' he said. 'Great-Gran thought you'd be needing some butter mebbe. She says that you've to ask for anything you need, and she'll be happy if you'd pay her a visit, tomorrow mebbe, if you've the time.'

'Oh, that's very sweet of her,' Carla smiled. 'I'd love to see her again.' She realised then that she had not yet made him and Tom known to one another, and she hastened to remedy the omission. 'Oh, Tom, this is another of what you're pleased to call the clan—Colin Hepburn. Colin, this is a friend of mine from London, Tom Laxey.'

They shook hands, but Tom was subjected to the same slightly suspicious regard from the son as he had been from the father, so that Carla wondered what there

was about him that aroused such suspicion in her relatives. 'I'll not stop,' Colin insisted, having dutifully exchanged formalities. 'We've the vet come to one of the
cows and I'd like to lend a hand. Mebbe learn something,' he added with a brief grin that relaxed the
schoolboy face for a moment.

Thinking she detected something more than simple
youthful curiosity, Carla smiled enquiringly. 'Are you
keen on veterinary work?' she asked, and noticed the
way Colin's young face took on a tight, closed look for
a moment.

'Aye,' he said. 'I'd like it fine if I could——'
He stopped there, even though Carla's expression
encouraged him to go on. 'You'd like to be a vet?' she
guessed, and knew she was right by the look in his eyes,
though his response barely confirmed it.

'Yes,' he said, but enlarged no further on the subject. 'I'll away back now, Carla, before the man leaves.'

Puzzled by something in his manner, Carla nodded
and smiled. 'Yes, all right, Colin.' She walked to the
door with him. 'I'll see you again later, I expect, if I
manage to get along and see your great-gran tomorrow.'

'Oh, and there was something else too,' Colin remembered as he stepped outside. 'She says to tell you
that she's spoken to Mrs Laurie from Gibbert in case
you're needing a hand with cleaning up the house.
She'll be along to see you.'

Carla smiled her thanks, although she was sorely
tempted to laugh aloud at old Annie's irrepressible
organising. Even though she was ninety-two years old
and seldom left the house any more, she still managed
to take a hand in most things that went on. But when
Carla turned back into the kitchen and went back to
cooking breakfast it was about Colin that she thought,
for his manner both troubled and puzzled her.

Tom bore the silence for several moments, then cocked an enquiring brow at her. 'Who *was* that?' he asked. 'Other than a sprig of the prolific Hepburn tribe?'

'Colin?' She turned to smile at him while she pushed bacon and eggs around in the huge frying pan. 'He's Alex's son, didn't I say?'

'No, you didn't.' Tom gave an exaggerated sigh of relief and smiled benignly at the slice of toast he had cooked to perfection. 'Well, I'm very glad to hear it.' Catching her curious glance, he laughed. 'I know women go for that strong silent type,' he said, 'and to be quite honest, love, I had the idea he might be—' he shrugged, '—a rival, so I'm very glad to discover he's a family man, safely married and blessed with children. It's a weight off my mind.'

Instead of looking at him, Carla concentrated on the contents of the frying pan, for they were almost cooked and in danger of spoiling if she allowed her attention to stray. Sliding two plates on to the table, she apportioned the bacon and eggs carefully between them while she answered him. 'Colin's mother died when he was born. In fact I don't think Alex knew her for all that long. She was only seventeen, I believe, and Alex was about twenty.'

'Ah-haa! Can it be that Cousin Alex was following in great-great-grandaddy's footsteps, then? Old Johnnie Hepburn, the notorious rake!'

Carla's swift shake of her head denied it without hesitation, and she was frowning without being aware that she did so. 'I was only about eight years old at the time,' she told him shortly, 'so I don't remember much about it. But he *did* marry her, so he wasn't like old Johnnie Hepburn in that way, if that's what you're getting at!'

Tom evidently decided to take warning from her

obvious dislike of the subject, and when he spoke again he carefully steered clear of any more insinuations. 'Isn't Colin at school?' he asked, and she shook her head.

'It's the long school holiday,' she reminded him. 'Normally he goes as a weekly boarder to a school in Gibbert. Old Annie's brought him up; just as she did Alex from the time he was thirteen, when his father died.'

Over his bacon and eggs, Tom looked up and beamed her a smile. 'She sounds a great character, your old Annie,' he said. 'Is there any chance of me meeting her while I'm here?'

Carla was unwilling to commit Annie to anything, and she did not see many strangers these days, so she trod cautiously. 'It's possible,' she allowed. 'But Annie doesn't see so many people now; mostly only family and people she's known for years.'

'Ah!'

He said no more on the subject. In fact they continued their meal without further mention of the Hepburn household, which was the way Carla preferred it. For one thing she felt rather self-conscious about springing so readily to Alex's defence, because without doubt Tom would have put his own construction on that. Alex was a subject she would prefer was not mentioned again yet awhile for, although she was not prepared to admit it openly, she feared that deep down in her heart somewhere the schoolgirlish dream she had once cherished still lingered.

It was when Carla noticed Tom's car heading along the road that lead to Hepburn's Carse that she rather belatedly wished she had warned him that the new road was not part of her property. No doubt that small branch road that turned away from the main one and stopped at the gate of Hepburn's Quay had been laid for the convenience of her grandfather, while Alex was having the rest done; he had been very fond of her grandfather always. But from the junction on was Alex's domain.

Probably no one would mind Tom driving on the road, as long as he remembered to close the mesh-link gate that was meant to keep the cattle from straying, but she would have been happier if he had stayed off what was to all intents Alex's property. At least for the time being.

Maybe, she thought, Tom did not intend going further than the gate, in which case she need not concern herself, and if he did she thought he was intelligent enough to realise that there were limits to the liberties one took, even with family-name properties. She was probably doing him an injustice by not trusting him automatically.

With other things in mind she got on with what she was doing. Tom might feel that there was time enough for cleaning up the old house and prefer to check the car, but Carla had different priorities. The more so because she wanted him to see just how impressive the place could look when it was clean and neat, as it had been in the old days.

The first hint she had of trouble was when she happened to glance out of one of the upstairs windows and noticed a thin straggle of red and white cattle nosing their inquisitive way out through the partly open gate, pausing only to nibble the grass by the roadside. Groaning inwardly, Carla dropped her duster and dashed for the stairs, running down them two at a time and almost coming to grief in her haste. In those few moments she would have screamed her anger at Tom if he had been available; as it was she saved her breath for the sprint she made along the garden path and out onto the road.

In too much haste to go right to the junction, she dashed across the grassland across the top of the loch. She was no countrywoman, and the idea of facing even a few stragglers made her legs tremble, but she dared not think what Alex would have to say if some of his precious herd got on to the public road, and that lent her both speed and courage. She had never run so fast in her life, and her breath was coming in great noisy gulps as she tore across the springy turf towards the road and the open gate.

Only about four or five animals were through the opening so far, but they were stupid creatures, and where one or two went the rest would follow sooner or later, and there must be several hundred head of cattle on the carse. She vaguely noticed Tom's car in the distance, going more slowly now, she thought, and then she noticed another figure racing with the same anxiety as herself for the gateway and the straying cattle.

On horseback Alex stood much more chance of arriving in time to stem the main flow, but Carla did not relax her own pace yet, not even when a sharp pain in her side warned her that she had already come too far, too fast. Tom must have realised too, for she saw the car turn tightly, almost in its own length, and come back towards the gate. Horse and car arrived at very nearly the same moment, and Carla could already hear voices raised when she slowed down and eventually stopped, holding her aching side and breathing hard, her heart thudding with the exhilaration of the chase.

She could not help but notice that Tom stayed in the car while Alex slid down from the big grey stallion he was riding, and drove the reluctant animals back inside the gate. By the time she had breath enough to go on and join them, they were already involved in a verbal battle, and from the way they both suddenly fell silent it was safe to assume that the language on both sides had been blisteringly angry.

Of the two Alex looked to be most in control of himself, although his anger smouldered like fury in the depth of those brown eyes and his mouth had a tight cruel look that sent little shivers down her back. Tom, probably as much guilt-stricken and defensive as angry, was the more garrulous of the two, though obviously it had not given him the upper hand.

'I'm sorry about this, Alex.' She gasped out the words before either of the men could say anything to her, and she looked at Alex with a certain wariness. He had a temper; she had grown up with the knowledge of that. All the Hepburns had tempers, it was part of their make-up. 'I should have warned Tom about shutting the gate, but I didn't think.'

His tall figure was taut with anger, and there was a tinglingly affecting aura about him that found a response in her own emotions. He had a right to be angry, she recognised it and sympathised with his point of view, but she was bound to stand by Tom in the present situation. He was the one so much out of his element here. The fact that she defended him, and took the blame on herself, however, brought a flush to Tom's good-looking features and he gave her a look that was reproachful as well as defensive.

'You don't have to make excuses for me, darling,' he told her, and from the corner of her eyes Carla saw Alex register that rather casual endearment. 'I left the damned gate open and I'm sorry about it, but it's a mistake anyone could make.'

'Did you think the gate was there for decoration only?' Alex demanded scathingly, then caught Carla's appealing look and chopped one big hand through the air impatiently. 'Och, town folks have little sense about such things! You'll do me the favour, Carla, of giving your friend a lesson on the country code, and remind

him that straying cattle can be costly—in more ways
than one!'

'Yes, I know, and I'm sorry about it, Alex.'

'Damn it, will you stop apologising for me as if I was
a naughty boy?' Tom demanded. 'I've already apolo-
gised for myself, and there's no need for you to go down
on your knees for me!' He turned on her and his eyes
were a sharp crackling blue she had never seen before.

'Tom, I'm not——'

'You'd better come back with me, sweetheart,' he
interrupted her, holding out a hand. 'You've run yourself into the ground, coming to the rescue of a few silly
cows.'

In fact she was breathing normally now, but her face
was flushed and warm and her hair wildly awry as she
pushed it back from her brow with the back of her
wrist. Conscious of Alex's eyes on her, steady and
gleamingly dark, she found herself looking at him
rather than at Tom, and the old responsive feelings
fluttered along her spine like moths responding to an
irresistible warmth.

'I recall you were aye fast on your feet,' he said,
almost cutting across Tom's rather waspish comment.
'You could run like a deer, I remember, with old
Donnie.'

It was almost as if he sought to remind Tom that the
two of them had a longer-standing relationship than
she had with Tom, and Carla was at a loss to know why
he bothered. The Hepburns were close, of course;
what Tom would call clannish, and it could simply be
Alex's way of reminding her that she was family.

Whatever his reason, it gave Carla a curiously warm
feeling to be reminded of a time before he went to
Canada, when he had noticed her running across the
carse in pursuit of her grandfather's old dog, bare legs
flashing and her hair flying out behind her, laughing

as she ran, with sheer happiness. A wild thing, Alex had called her that time, and she had thought he disapproved, and been unhappy as a consequence. For she had been only sixteen at the time and she had adored him.

'Shall we go back?' Tom's voice recalled her, and she did not look at Alex again, though she was aware of him remounting the big grey horse and holding him in check for a moment while he looked down at her and Tom together.

'Remember!' he said shortly, and put his heels to the animal's sides with such force that he leapt into action.

'Surly devil!' muttered Tom, just as he had the first time he and Alex met. Carla said nothing, but silently shook her head.

Carla did not manage to get over to see Annie Hepburn as she had hoped, but she promised herself she would go the following day, as soon as she had done all the necessary jobs in the house. Tom was outside somewhere, probably tinkering with the car again. He was a town man born and bred, and the very idea of being several miles from the nearest garage made him mildly neurotic about keeping the car in good order.

Hearing the sound of an engine close by, Carla guessed he had brought the car round to the side of the house, and she looked up when she heard footsteps on the path. Expecting to see Tom, she stared uncomprehendingly for a few seconds when she realised that it was Alex and not Tom who came striding along the overgrown path to the house, and her heart was banging urgently while she sought for reasons for his being there.

He looked purposeful and a little tense, she thought, and wondered if there was to be any come-back about

yesterday's incident with the gate left open and the
cattle straying. She hoped not, for all their sakes. He
had arrived in a Land-Rover this morning, but he was
dressed much the same as he had been yesterday, and
his stride emphasised the length of his legs and the
lean graceful lines of his body.

She greeted him from the partly open kitchen window, smiling a welcome even though she felt vaguely
suspicious of his reason for being there. Alex would not
be paying a social visit to Hepburn's Quay now that
her grandfather was no longer there, she was almost
sure.

'Good morning, Alex—come in!'

Vaguely she noticed that he was already ducking in
through the doorway before she actually issued the invitation, and it reminded her that he was in fact far
more familiar with the old house than she was herself,
and had been in the habit of calling on her grandfather
when he was alive, much more frequently than she had
been able to do.

For the moment he stayed in the doorway, with one
hand on the jamb, the arm raised to support him and
his steady brown eyes regarding her, seeming to question her without giving a hint of what he wanted to
know. Then he glanced around the big kitchen and
made it clear that he was content to find her alone.

Anxious to clear the air, Carla came immediately to
his reason for being there. 'I hope you haven't come to
complain further about that business yesterday,' she
told him, and there was a suggestion of challenge in the
way she looked at him.

'That's over and forgotten,' he declared, but immediately qualified it by adding, 'as long as it doesn't
happen again.'

'It won't,' Carla assured him firmly. 'Tom isn't an
idiot, he just didn't stop to think.' She eyed him for a

moment, leaving him in no doubt that she knew better than to suppose he was simply paying a social call. 'What *have* you come to see me about, Alex? I know it isn't just to be social.'

'Oh, you do?' His eyes held hers for just a moment, then Carla found it too discomforting and looked away. 'I came to see you about the matter I mentioned earlier, you remember? I'm glad to find you alone.'

Something, Carla had no idea what, prompted her to let him know that Tom was close by. 'I'm not really,' she said. 'Tom's outside in the old byre, checking on the car.'

'Hmm.' Apparently he would have preferred Tom at a greater distance, but he was not deterred completely. 'Well, no matter, I'll say what I have to say, now I'm here.'

He gave the impression of having little time to spare, but he accepted her invitation to sit down at the kitchen table with her, and crossed one leg over the other, apparently at ease for all his air of urgency. 'Will you have coffee?' she asked, and flushed when he shook his head impatiently.

'No, thanks, I just came to see you about Hepburn's Quay.'

'This place?' Carla frowned at him curiously. 'I don't get your meaning, Alex. What about Hepburn's Quay? There's no quibble about my right to it—Grampy had no other grandchildren, and my mother was his only child.'

A large brown hand dismissed any doubts concerning her claim, but Carla resented his obvious impatience and her expression showed it. 'I don't dispute your right to it as your inheritance,' he said. 'But when I talked to Uncle Fergus about it, he said you'd be prepared to sell it to me. After all,' he went on when he saw how she looked, 'this isn't the kind of life you're used to, Carla, and you can't really want to live here. What would you do? You and your—friend?'

The inference of that slight pause was so unmistakable that Carla momentarily pushed aside the reason for his errand and took him up on the matter of herself and Tom. She had blushed like a schoolgirl and now she squirmed inwardly because she knew he would have noted the fact. 'Tom is a *good* friend,' she insisted, unconscious in the first instance of having added fuel to the fire by stressing the fact so insistently. 'And I hope he'll remain one.'

'Oh?' Brown eyes regarded her with a hint of suspicion. 'You'll not be thinking of marrying him, then?'

The subject was too personal for Carla to discuss it with any degree of coolness, although she did her best. In the circumstances she almost wished Tom was there to lend her moral support, although he was unlikely to have taken Alex's remarks with as much restraint as she was trying to.

'No,' she said firmly. 'We're not getting married—at least not at the moment.'

'Ah, I see.'

Again the implication was too blatant to overlook and, as before, Carla resented it bitterly. She was glaring at him in a way she would never have imagined herself doing where Alex was concerned. 'I don't think you see at all,' she told him, keeping her voice firmly under control, but Alex was taking note of two lots of breakfast dishes that she had not yet had time to dispose of.

'I see that you're living under the same roof,' he said. 'It's not so unusual for a man and woman to dispense with the formality of marriage if they've no mind for it, but you cannot blame anyone for noticing, Carla. And you're gey touchy about it, it seems to me.'

Carla was having difficulty controlling her temper, and it blazed in her eyes until they looked the colour of emeralds. She had never, ever visualised herself being angry with Alex, especially as bitterly angry as she was at the moment, and she struggled hard to control her anger, though with little success.

'Of course I'm touchy about it,' she told him furiously, 'because it isn't true! If you can tell me an alternative to us being under the same roof, as you term it, I'll be happy to satisfy your puritan soul, Alex! There isn't an hotel within miles of here, and I don't fancy staying here alone while Tom goes off into Gibbert and stays at the pub, so we're both under the same roof!'

'Did you not think about coming to stay at the Carse?' Alex enquired. 'We've plenty of room, and you could both have been accommodated easily.'

She hadn't thought about it and probably, she thought ruefully, her expression told him as much. But she was in no mind to yield to his arguments now. 'Hepburn's Quay is mine and I wanted to stay here,' she insisted. 'I know Annie would have put us up if I'd asked her, but I preferred to come to the Quay.'

'With your—friend. Aye, well, it's understandable in that case.'

His very coolness was an added irritant to Carla, and she did not altogether understand her own furious emotions. She had never, in her countless dreams of one day meeting Alex again, anticipated their coming close to quarrelling, but she could not let him get away with his insinuations unchecked. 'If you'd care to go upstairs and check for yourself, you'll see that there were two bedrooms used last night, not one!'

For the moment Alex said nothing, but he was not nearly as non-plussed as Carla felt he ought to have been. Then she noticed that just briefly the corners of his mouth twitched in a suggestion of a smile and he shook his head. 'I never knew you had the Hepburn temper, Carla; you were always such a meek and mild wee missie when you came here before.'

'I was never meek and mild!' Carla denied it swiftly while she tried to do something to control the beat of her heart. 'But I was only seventeen when you saw me last, and I'm a competent adult now, in full possession of all my faculties and used to standing on my own feet! I don't take kindly to having my morals questioned, even if you are some kind of distant cousin and probably think you have the right to question me! If that's all you came for, to preach me a lesson on morals, Alex, you can go—now!'

'All right, all right!' He was on his feet, the same Hepburn temper sparking dark gleaming lights in his eyes. 'I came to talk business with you, not indulge in a slanging match! God, woman, can you not give me the chance to say what I came to say?'

Carla was trembling like a leaf, shattered by emotions she had never known before, but she faced him with the determination firmly in her heart, not to let him get under her skin any more than he already had. 'What *did* you want to say?' she asked. 'Something about Grampy telling you I'd sell Hepburn's Quay to you? Well, I won't, Alex. I've no intention of selling the Quay to anyone.'

Quite clearly it was not what he expected, and his frown indicated uncertainty as well as displeasure, Carla suspected. Alex was confident and bold, used to going his own way, and she could imagine her grandfather discussing the matter with him, for they had been good friends always. She had no reason to suppose he was not telling the truth about it.

She could easily imagine her grandfather explaining that Carla was his only grandchild and that he was

bound to leave Hepburn's Quay to her. But she could
just as easily imagine him nodding wisely and saying
that he knew wee Carla wouldn't want the old place to
live in. He, Alex, could talk the lassie round to his way
of thinking once the house was hers. He would be sure
of it, for the old man had been wise and observant
enough to notice how she had adored Alex during
those brief summer visits.

'I—I have a use for it,' she explained, less aggressive
now because thinking about her grandfather had
weakened her anger. 'I'm sorry, Alex, but I don't want
to sell.'

He stood beside the table, looming big even in the
vast kitchen, and with one hand thrust into a pocket,
his eyes on her but veiled by thick lashes—an unexpectedly feminine characteristic in such a very masculine man. 'May I ask what you plan to do with it?' he
asked. 'It's surely too big for two people, although I
know it's not had any but Uncle Fergus here for the
last sixteen years. What do you plan to do with it,
Carla?'

She could have told him it was no concern of his, and
been within her rights, she supposed. But it was hard
not to respond to that deep quiet voice with its accent
so reminiscent of her grandfather's, only a little less
pronounced. 'I—we're considering turning it into an
hotel,' she said. 'Just a small and very exclusive hotel.'

'You're not serious?' He did not raise his voice, but
Carla looked up at him and frowned. 'You'll not be
seriously considering making the Quay into an hotel?
It wasn't *your* idea, of course?'

Stung to her own defence once more, Carla frowned.
'As a matter of fact it *was* my idea,' she told him.
'Although Tom was quick to see the possibilities when
I told him. He even offered to come in as a partner if
the house was suitable. That's why he came all this

way with me, to see if it *is* suitable.'

'And you think it is?'

Carla did not even know that herself yet, and she was much too unsure of Tom's opinion to answer very confidently. 'He—we haven't decided for certain yet, but I think he's quite favourably impressed.'

His expression showed how doubtful he was about it, and he did not hesitate to say as much. 'It's too small and too run down,' he said, and she angled her chin warningly.

'That's for Tom to decide!'

He frowned suspiciously. 'Who is he, Carla?' he asked bluntly. 'How long have you known him? You're not a staggeringly wealthy heiress, I know, but you've enough from your grandfather to make you a fair target for some limmer with an eye to the main chance.'

Carla stared at him in silence, too staggered for the moment to even object, but listening to the loud urgent throbbing of the pulse at her temple, increasing in urgency every second. She never quite knew how she managed it, but somehow she kept control of her temper and spoke in a small tight voice, while her eyes watched him steadily, bright and angrily green.

'Tom's no fortune-hunter,' she told him. 'His father owns a very successful export business in London, and I worked for him until a few days ago. If you suspect anyone of fortune-hunting, it had better be me, because what I have from Grampy is a drop in the ocean compared to the amount Tom is able—and willing—to invest in Hepburn's Quay!'

Even now Alex was not put out, Carla realised. She was trembling with the force of her own emotions, but he merely nodded his head slowly, then met her eyes with the same bold confidence as before. 'Just as long as he's not a wrong 'un,' he said, 'that's all right. But we had to be sure, Carla.'

'Is that the royal "we" you're using?' she asked, but regretted the sarcasm the moment it passed her lips.

Alex's gaze never wavered, and she felt so small and mean that she wished she could sink through the floor. Of course old Annie and her family would be anxious that she should not be duped by a stranger, and Alex no less than his grandmother and his aunts. 'I meant all of us,' he told her. 'You're not such a worldly-wise woman that you cannot be duped, Carla.'

Shaking her head, she kept her eyes downcast. 'I'm sorry, it's just that I'm rather—touchy,' she said. 'But you've nothing to concern yourselves about, Alex. I've known Tom for more than a year, and he's a nice ordinary sort of man that no family need worry about. He's offered to come in as a partner if he thinks the Quay is suitable for an hotel, and if not——' She shrugged, because she did not know what was going to happen if her plans did not materialise. She had not thought that far yet. Then something else occurred to her, and she looked up at him curiously. 'What did *you* want it for?'

'Staff quarters.' He noticed her puzzled frown and went on to explain. 'I need more men now that the ranch—the farm is expanding and running well and I need somewhere to house the men I bring in. The Quay would be taken into the Carse estate and make up a whole.'

'In other words you want to use it as the equivalent of the cowboy-style bunkhouse?' she guessed dryly. 'I don't think Grampy agreed to that idea, Alex, did he?'

'Aye, he did! Only he used his head and knew I'd make living quarters for married men!'

Carla looked uneasy, for it would seem he and her grandfather had really put their heads together, and it was harder refusing when she knew Grampy had approved his scheme. 'Then I'm sorry I don't see eye to

eye with Grampy's ideas for once,' she told him. 'I
visualise something better than that for the old house.'

'An hotel!' He shook his head as if he could imagine
no worse fate for any house, and made his way to the
door again with Carla following after him and not at-
tempting to keep pace with his long stride. 'You'll
never make a go of it, Carla! The amount you'll have
to lay out to make it acceptable to the kind of clients
you obviously have in mind, won't balance with the
number of rooms you'll have here. You cannot make a
go of it, I'll stake my life on it!'

He turned in the doorway and faced her once more,
and the move was so unexpected that she stepped back
hastily when she found herself too close on his heels
for comfort. For a second or two they had collided and
there was a curiously breathtaking sensation in the
contact, brief as it was.

'You don't know that,' she challenged, with an unmistakable shiver in her voice. 'You made a go of your
ranch from virtually nothing, so I don't see why you
doubt my ability to make a success of Hepburn's Quay
as an hotel! I'm a Hepburn as well, you know, and
just as determined and capable of hard work as you
are!'

The sun fell in a slanting beam across her face as she
stood in the doorway, catching deep warm glints of
auburn in her hair and giving a soft golden glow to her
city-pale skin. She could sense the same deep-running
passion for possession in Alex that stirred in herself,
and it brought with it a strange and exhilarating excitement.

But it was completely unexpected when her arms
were gripped by hard strong fingers suddenly and she
was swung round until her face was in the full glare of
the sun. She was momentarily blinded by it, so that she
felt rather than saw the looming shadow of a dark face

over her, looking directly into her eyes.

'Green eyes!' Alex declared in a thick, rough voice
that breathed warm against her lips. 'Green-eyed
women are aye stubborn, so they say, but there's ways
of taming stubborn wee creatures like you, Carla ma
girl, and yon man you've brought with you is not the
one to do it, I'm thinking!' She squirmed in his hold,
but too late. His mouth was already on hers, fierce and
hard, but brief in its touch; then he laughed shortly
and thrust her back into the doorway before he went
striding off down the path. 'Goodbye, cousin!'

It seemed such a long time since Carla had visited
Hepburn's Carse, and it had changed more than she
imagined. Not so much the house, but the surroundings. The house still stood bland and mellow amid its
clusters of gorse and rowans, with only a few straggling
rose trees and a may tree to suggest anything of a
flower-garden. Far more important was the area given
over to the cultivation of fruit and vegetables, which
had always been old Annie Hepburn's pride and joy.

She had never forgotten her early days as a crofter's
daughter, when food, or lack of it, had taken prece-
dence over everything else. Even nearly eighty years of
comparative plenty had not blunted her instinct for
utilising every inch of ground for growing food, rather
than growing flowers for the pleasure of their beauty.

Neat, white ranch-type fences were new to Carla, and
she thought they brought a slightly rakish air to the
place, but the character of the old house still domin-
ated even its modernised surroundings. The reason for
the white fencing became clearer when Carla got
closer to it, for it formed a paddock for several young
horses, frisky and energetic in the warm sun. Another
of Alex's innovations, she guessed; he had always been
fond of horses and breeding thoroughbreds would be a

profitable addition to his already thriving ranch-type farm.

She spent a moment or two admiring the horses before she made her way to the house, but she saw no one about, even as she started up the four steps to the front door. It stood ajar and she peered inside the big hall, one hand widening the gap slightly; only then did she hear any sign of life.

From across the hall, coming from what she knew to be the family sitting-room, she heard voices. It would have been difficult not to hear them, in fact, for they were raised in anger, and she hesitated before using the hefty brass knocker to announce her arrival. Alex's voice was easily recognised, and so was Colin's, wavering between a boy's treble and a man's deeper pitch, and cracking uncertainly as it rose in anger. But it was old Annie Hepburn's thin but firm tone that took charge while Carla still hesitated.

'You'll be quiet, the two of ye! D'ye hear me?' Annie always became much more broad when she was roused, and seemingly some kind of family quarrel was in progress. 'Now you go about your business with the beasties, Alex,' she ordered, 'and you, ma laddie, you get to your books. Just because yon school's closed is no reason for neglecting your learning! Away now and do as I say, the pair of ye! I'll not have feuding in my house—aye, an' it's *still* mine, for a' you have the running of the land, Alex! Away now, the two o' ye!'

There was never any doubt that she would be obeyed, even by her strong-minded grandson, and because the silence that followed her instruction forewarned of someone coming out and finding her there, Carla raised her hand and thudded the brass knocker on the door two or three times in succession. She waited, her heart hammering hard in her breast, for without her being aware of the reason for it, it alarmed her to hear the Hepburns quarrelling among themselves.

Colin emerged first, but he did no more than glance in her direction before darting up the staircase that faced the front door. He was close to tears, Carla suspected when she caught a glimpse of mistiness in his grey eyes and noticed how his bottom lip trembled. Alex came close on his heels, and the frown that drew his brows into a straight line above eyes that glittered like agates did not change a jot when he saw her.

He had on the same fawn trousers, with a white shirt that was already showing signs of having been worn for some heavy labour that made it cling moistly to his body like a second skin; and he signalled to her with an impatient hand as he came across the hall towards her, inviting her in.

She obeyed, stepping inside the hall and venturing a vague smile by way of greeting; finding it difficult to forget that brief, hard unforgettable kiss, now that she saw him again. Being kissed by Alex was a new enough experience to have aroused those embarrassing, girlish memories again, and she wanted very much to ignore it, because making an issue of it would simply endow it with too much importance.

'Hello again, Alex,' she greeted him coolly. 'Is it convenient for me to see Annie now?'

'Come away in,' Alex bade her brusquely, and glanced over his shoulder at the door he had left open in the sitting-room. 'Mebbe you can soothe her ruffled feathers; I've neither the time nor the patience at the moment!'

He paid no heed to her familiar use of his grandmother's name, for no one but her immediate family called her anything but Annie, and it was no cause for offence, no matter how her years advanced. But she looked at Alex curiously, taking a chance on being

snubbed to try and discover what it was that had
ruffled the old lady's feathers in the first place. If she
was being asked to restore her to good humour, she felt
entitled to know what had upset her.

'What's the matter? What's upset her, Alex?'

He fixed his brown eyes on her for a moment in a
way that suggested he was pretty sure she had overheard at least the last part of their quarrel, but he did
not attempt to enlighten her about its cause. Instead
he merely shrugged impatiently and eased past her in
the doorway, his taut lean body brushing close until
she moved further inside to let him past.

'Och, it's some nonsense of young Colin's!' he said.
'Mebbe you can talk some sense into him as well while
you're here! God knows I can't get through to him!'

'Is it because he wants to be a——'

Her words trailed off when she was caught by the
suddenly narrowed glitter of his eyes. She did not even
know whether Colin had confided his ambition to his
family yet, and she could be breaking a confidence. But
Alex was not prepared to let it rest there, and his
always firm mouth was tight and straight, almost cruel,
while he watched her closely.

'Go on,' he said softly. 'You seem to be pretty well
informed, considering you've not been here five
minutes!'

Stung by his attitude of suspicion, Carla flushed,
tilting her chin a little as she looked up at him. 'I asked
Colin, when he came yesterday, if he wanted to be a vet.
He spoke about the vet being here to see one of the
cows, and he wanted to get back and help him, and it
seemed a logical enough conclusion to draw. I don't
see that it's so unreasonable an ambition for a boy who
lives on a farm.'

'Oh, you don't?'

'No, of course I don't!' She knew she had given him

the wrong answer, but she was not going to retract a single word she had said, and she defied him to expect it. 'What's wrong with being a vet?'

Alex was silent for a moment, looking down at her bright defiant eyes and flushed cheeks, and obviously fuming inwardly. Then he turned abruptly away and called to her over one shoulder as he went down the front steps two at a time. 'Och, away in and ask my grandmother!' he advised shortly.

Left with little alternative but to do as he said, Carla found old Annie Hepburn alone in the big family sitting-room. Hepburn's Carse was no bigger than her own newly inherited property, but it had never known the loneliness of a solitary old man living on his own. It had always been a family house, and it suffered none of the neglect that gave such an air of sadness to Hepburn's Quay.

Of seven children, Annie Hepburn had had only one son, Alex's father, but her six daughters had families and provided her with a constant stream of grandchildren and great-grandchildren, all of whom were fairly frequent visitors. It was the family atmosphere that gave the house its warm expansive air that not even that explosive quarrel could disturb.

Annie was a matriarch and enjoyed the role, playing it to the full. She did not look her ninety-two years, and even now retained traces of the beauty that had earned her the nickname of Bonnie Annie McClure. Until Robert Hepburn, one of the notorious Johnnie's grandsons, had come along and changed both her name and her circumstances.

She smiled when she saw Carla, and the anger in her bright dark eyes faded in the few moments it took her visitor to walk across the room to her. She had a great pride and interest in all the Hepburns, no matter how

distant the relationship. 'Carla! Come away in, hein,
and let me see you! I can't see more than five feet away
now without I've my spectacles on and I can never find
the things when I need them!' She held Carla at arm's
length and subjected her to an almost embarrassingly
close scrutiny. Smiling and nodding over smooth pink
cheeks and a soft full mouth; green eyes set between
reddish-brown lashes, and the whole small heart shape
framed with the unmistakable Hepburn hair, thick and
fox-red and very slightly curling. 'Och, you're a bonny
sight,' she approved, and drew her close to kiss her
cheek. 'A bonny sight.'

'It seems an awful long time since I saw you, Annie.'
Inevitably, Carla knew, the conversation would come
around to her grandfather, and she would as soon it
was over quickly because she could still become tearful
if the subject was dwelt on over-long. 'I—I wanted to
come for Grampy's funeral,' she explained, 'but I
couldn't. I had 'flu and I couldn't travel.'

'Aye, I know, I know.' Thin hands soothed hers
gently, and there was gentleness now in the bright dark
eyes. 'Puir Fergus, he was a gey lonely man those last
sixteen years after his Marie went, and I doubt not he
was glad to go to his Maker. Let that comfort you,
child.'

Carla coped with threatening tears, anxious to have
the subject ended before she made a fool of herself.
'I—I miss him a lot at the Quay, Annie, but I'm trying
not to let it get me down.'

'That's best,' old Annie approved, again patting her
hand. 'And you've a friend there with ye, to take your
mind off it, I hear.'

Guessing the source of her information, Carla smiled
wryly. 'Alex told you,' she guessed, and looked surprised when the old lady shook her head.

'It was Colin told me,' she said. 'Alex has not said

a word about it. You'd think the man didn't exist for all he's told me!'

Not over-anxious to dwell on Alex's reasons for keeping quiet about Tom's presence at Hepburn's Quay, Carla went on to talk about Colin's visit. 'I was amazed to see how much Colin's grown in the past year,' she said. 'He's taller than I am now, but I suppose he'll be taking O-levels next year, won't he? Will he be staying on after that?'

'Och, who's to tell?' Annie asked with a touch of asperity. 'Yon two limmers will see me in the mad house with their to-ing and fro-ing! One says this and the other says something other—it's those years that Alex was away, ye ken. Colin was no more than nine when he went and now he sees himself as near a grown man; or he did until Alex came home last year. He resents Alex behaving like a father after all this time, and he lets his father know it!'

Carla shrugged, vaguely apologetic. 'I couldn't help overhearing the tail-end of a quarrel when I arrived,' she confessed, 'and when I saw Alex in the hall he looked as if he'd like to murder somebody.'

'He's the Hepburn temper,' Annie said, but not without a certain curious pride in the fact. 'But Colin's got the stubbornness. And although they don't often come as near to blows as just now, they get gey fierce sometimes and I'm hard-put to keep the peace. Young Colin has his mind set on being a vet just now, and Alex is putting his foot down hard about it.'

'But why should he?' Carla asked. Her sympathies were with Colin so far, and Alex's objections not only puzzled her but struck her as unreasonable.

'Can you not see?' old Annie asked her with a hint of sadness. 'A man doesn't build up a place like this to leave to anyone but his son. All this hard work and planning that's gone into making the Carse what it is now, all the new methods he learned while he was in Canada, and is making work here. It was all done for Colin—so that he could come into a rich inheritance when his father's gone.'

Carla could see it then, and she felt her loyalties divided. For while she could see how bitter it must be for Alex to have put so much into the estate, to build it into a miniature empire for his son, only to have it rejected, she could also see Colin's point of view in wanting to follow his own inclinations. She could imagine how hard it was for the old lady too, having to keep a balance between the two of them, and probably seeing, as Carla did, both sides with equal clarity, but so much more closely involved in both their lives than Carla was.

'Ah, well,' said Annie, breaking into her sympathetic musings, 'ye've not come here to listen to our troubles, hein, have you? Tell me what you plan to do yourself. Will you be staying a wee while at the Quay, you and your friend?'

Apparently Alex had not even told her that much, and Carla found it harder to tell Annie her plans for Hepburn's Quay than it had been to tell Alex. She could be almost certain that Annie knew about the arrangement her grandfather had with Alex, and she would be as taken aback to learn that there had been a change of plan as he had been. None of the Hepburns took kindly to having their plans thwarted, not even those who were only Hepburns by marriage, as Annie was.

As briefly and explicitly as she could in the circumstances, Carla laid out her scheme for an hotel, and she knew before she had finished speaking that for the first time in her life, she had incurred the old lady's displeasure. The bright dark eyes gleamed, and searched her face with an intensity that reminded her of Alex.

'An hotel?' She said it in much the same way he had. 'Do you not know, girl, that your granddaddy arranged for Alex to have the Quay when he was gone?'

Carla's cheeks flushed and she stood her ground, no matter how strange it felt, no longer being in that warm glow of approval. 'Grampy left the Quay to me, Annie; I know nothing about an arrangement, except what Alex told me this morning.'

'And you think he'd lie to you, girl?' Carla shook her head. 'But you'd break a man's word when he's no longer here to make it good? What kind o' limmer is yon man you've brought with you if he makes ye put aside sworn promises? Och, think on it, girl! The Quay's run down, damp, it needs a fair bit of money spent on it, and I doubt you've the means to make it more than a wee guest house place, that'll ruin ye in a year or less! Let Alex have it, as he was promised, and ye'll not regret it. He'll pay well, and he was aye fond of ye, ye ken that.'

That was news to Carla, and she suspected the information was merely a ploy of old Annie's to gain ground for her beloved grandson. Alex wanted Hepburn's Quay, and she would do her best to see that he got it, however she went about it. But Carla had one advantage, she was in possession of the Quay, quite legally, and for the moment that was how it stood. Also she had the Hepburn stubbornness, just as Alex had said.

'I'm sorry, Annie.' She clasped her hands tightly together, because she genuinely *was* sorry. Partly, she realised, because it would have pleased Alex if she had been ready to let him have the house, but also because she did not like being at odds with his formidable grandmother. 'I have my heart set on this scheme,' she explained, in the vain hope of it making a difference to her attitude. 'I have at least to try and make a go of it.'

'You were aye fond of Alex,' Annie recalled, cunningly aware that it was a fact Carla could hardly deny. 'Were he to marry again, lassie, it might well be you he married, then the Quay would be his anyway. Have ye thought on that?'

She watched the flush that mounted Carla's cheeks and smiled knowingly. 'I think you're taking a lot for granted, Annie,' was all Carla could think of in the way of protest, and her voice was curiously breathless.

'D'ye not think I've seen the way ye looked at Alex whenever ye were here each summer, girl?' the old lady persisted. 'He's needing a wife, God knows, and I'd as soon he married one of our ain kind as some brassy outsider. You'd like fine to be married to Alex, would you not, child?'

Almost too embarrassed to be angry, Carla took a firm hold on her self-control, but even so her voice trembled far more than she hoped it would, and as she so often did when she was emotionally upset, she got to her feet. 'I probably did have a schoolgirl crush on Alex, years ago,' she said. 'But that's all past now, Annie, and I'm seriously considering marrying Tom, the friend who drove me up here from London. He's asked me, and it's quite likely I'll say yes.'

She was treading on dangerously unknown ground there, Carla realised, but she had spoken hastily in self-defence. Although she had nursed that youthful passion for Alex all those years ago, she had never realised how obvious it had been to others, and she was appalled at the idea of it having been just as evident to Alex himself. Casting Tom as possible husband would at least help to demolish any lingering ideas that she still worshipped Alex.

'D'ye tell me that?' old Annie enquired with deceptive mildness. 'Well, we'll see, I dare say, all in good time.' She looked at Carla's flushed and embarrassed face and shook her head. 'But you'll not be running off so soon when we've not said half a dozen words together, surely?' she added. 'Sit down again and we'll have a nice long yammer. Come, girl—sit down!'

She was so adamant that Carla obeyed because there was little else she could do. But she vowed not to mention either Alex or marriage again while she was there. And certainly not in the same breath.

CHAPTER THREE

CARLA wished she knew what Tom's final decision was likely to be. He had still not committed himself to a definite yes or no concerning the use of Hepburn's Quay, and she felt very much in the air, waiting to discover if the old house was to eventually become an hotel, or simply prove to be a white elephant that she might just as well have let Alex buy from her as he wanted to. Without Tom's financial help she could not manage, she had already faced that fact.

This was their fourth day at the Quay, and they had managed to make living a bit more comfortable. Bedrooms had been aired and they had done some household shopping in Gibbert, the nearest town, but it was clear that the onus of their domestic arrangements was going to fall on Carla's shoulders. for Tom was a complete novice in that direction. It was through Tom that she lost the opportunity of Mrs Laurie's services too.

When the woman old Annie had recommended to help clean up arrived as promised, Tom had told her that she was not needed, and she left again, bristling with indignation. Faced with cleaning the place from top to bottom virtually single-handed, Carla had demanded to know what his idea was, and he had promptly informed her that he was not happy at the thought of having one of Annie Hepburn's cronies in the house, and probably reporting back to the old lady. No amount of persuasion could make him change his mind, and they had come as near to quarrelling as they had ever done—even though he promised to find a replacement.

In the meantime, Carla did what she could herself, occasionally giving Tom something to do that he could do unsupervised. But six months' neglect made for a great deal of work, and she was not feeling very charitable towards Tom as she swept and dusted the sitting-room that had seldom been used since her grandmother died, sixteen years before. It was all very well for Tom, he had driven into Gibbert for several items they needed, including the daily newspaper and petrol for the car, but she was the one doing all the work.

She glanced up when she heard the car return and head for the old cow-byre at the rear of the house that Tom had decided would serve as a garage. Then she listened absently to sounds that told her he had yet again bumped the offside wing of the car on the doorway. He would be annoyed about it, but it would not last very long; Tom's moods never did.

She was in the kitchen when he came in and she looked up, her guess about the car confirmed by a slight frown between his brows. 'Did you get everything?' she asked quickly, forestalling the inevitable moan about the byre entrance being too narrow, and he flopped down on to a kitchen chair before he answered.

'I hope so.' He blew out an exaggerated breath. 'I have to get used to this living in the middle of nowhere; take a survival course or something, or I shall very likely perish from sheer ignorance.'

From across the table Carla looked at him, and wondered yet again if he was already having second thoughts. If his decision about Hepburn's Quay was more likely to be influenced by his dislike of the unaccustomed isolation than by the unsuitability of the old house. If he was having second thoughts it would be only fair to give him the opportunity of getting out before he became any more deeply involved, even though it meant the end of her own plans. After all, she had had some prior knowledge of the conditions, but Tom had come into it solely on her say-so.

'Tom,' she ventured, 'you're not regretting having come into this—this business, are you? I mean, if you are——'

'If I am, darling, you'll be the first to know.' He stretched out and took one of her hands, squeezing it hard. 'I'm still deciding, I promise you. It's just that I'm such a town-bird that I have to acclimatise myself before I can make a fair assessment.' An amiable grin assured her it was true and once more made her aware of just how good-looking he was. 'You may not realise it, my lovely, but I've never been anywhere more primitive than the beach at St Tropez before—I'm not your strong, silent outdoor type, you know.'

Carla ignored the obvious allusion to Alex, and continued to study him, not completely convinced. 'It's just that I don't want you getting into something you're going to regret.'

Tom got up from his chair and walked around the table to slide an arm around her waist, bending to kiss her cheek lightly as he did so. When he spoke his breath warmed her cheek and sent pleasant little thrills of sensation fluttering over her skin. 'I don't get into anything I'm likely to regret, my dear, don't worry,' he assured her, and his confidence reminded her yet again that he was an astute businessman. Despite his personal interest in her, he would never lose sight of the practicalities. 'If the scheme doesn't stand a chance of working, I shan't get involved, and I'll take care that you don't either. That's a promise—O.K.?'

Carla nodded, satisfied up to a point, but wondering what was going to happen to Hepburn's Quay if the hotel idea fell through. She could not see herself eating humble pie to the extent of offering it to Alex after all, and yet she could think of no other alternative at the moment. 'O.K.,' she agreed. 'Did you get the paper while you were out?'

'Oh, damn!'

His look of dismay was so exaggerated that she laughed. 'Oh well, it doesn't really matter if we don't know what's going on in the rest of the world, I suppose.'

'I could phone and——' He stopped, eyeing her curiously. '*Is* there a phone handy?'

'Only at the Carse,' Carla told him. 'Grampy never had one put in.'

Tom pulled a face. 'So your fierce kinsmen have charge of our only link with civilisation?' Carla nodded, letting the allusion pass for the moment, and Tom went on, with such studied carelessness that she was immediately suspicious. 'Incidentally,' he said, 'I saw your cousin Alex in the village.'

Gibbert was in fact a small town, but Tom was a Londoner and to him anywhere as small as Gibbert was a village, and Carla was far too distracted to bother correcting him. 'Oh yes?' She meticulously dusted the edge of the kitchen dresser while she spoke. 'He was shopping, I suppose, like you were.'

There was a gleam in Tom's eyes and he twitched his brows in a way that was clearly meant to convey more than the words he spoke. 'If he was, he knows where the bargains are! This particular package was blonde and beautiful and about thirty years old, wrapped in a mink that must have set somebody back a small fortune, I would guess. Does cousin Alex have that kind of money?'

Carla ignored the question but struggled for a moment with an unexpected surge of emotion. Her pulse was hammering hard and her hands seemed incredibly clumsy as she moved various items on the

dresser and dusted underneath them. 'Annie did hint
that there was somebody. A brassy outsider, she said,'
she recalled with unconscious malice. 'Maybe that's
who it was.'

'Maybe.' Tom was watching her, she sensed it even
though she had her back to him, and she rued that
malicious quote already. Maybe Tom himself felt a
tinge of envy for Alex's conquest, for he had a taste
for beautiful women and, except for Carla, his women
friends were invariably wealthy too. 'I wouldn't have
called her brassy, though,' he mused, and obviously
had little trouble recalling the woman in question.
'She was smooth and beautiful and very expensive, but
not brassy, although I suppose old Annie would take
a biased view if cousin Alex has it in mind to bring
her home as a bride.'

Carla took a firm hold on her own prejudices and
refused to recognise the fact that she would dislike any
female that Alex Hepburn fancied, as a matter of
course. 'Naturally it matters to Annie who Alex mar-
ries,' she told Tom. 'The Carse is still hers, strictly
speaking, and whoever the woman is she needs to—fit
in.'

Tom was perched on the edge of the table just behind
her. 'Like you would?' he suggested quietly, but Carla
said nothing. 'That *is* what the old lady would like,
isn't it, Carla? I mean, there is—was some kind of—
understanding about it, wasn't there?'

'There was *no* understanding!' She denied it firmly,
but as much to convince herself as to convince Tom.
There had been no understanding; only a kind of wild,
hopeless longing on her side, because he always seemed
so unattainable.

Tom turned her to face him, his hands at her waist.
'What is there with you two, then, Carla? There's
something,' he insisted before she could deny it. 'I

sensed it when he came up and spoke to us the first day we were here.'

'There's nothing.' She kept her eyes downcast, discounting that brief, impulsive kiss of Alex's, and old Annie's assurance that he had always been fond of her, and shook her head firmly. 'I've known Alex all my life, on and off through various summer holidays I've spent here, except for the five years he spent in Canada, and of course he's related, distantly. Maybe——' She hesitated, reluctant to go on, shrugging her shoulders in a way that was meant to appear uncaring but instead seemed merely resigned. 'When I was a schoolgirl I had a silly crush on Alex. He was a lot older than me, and a widower with a child, but you know what young girls are like—I was only seventeen when I saw him last. Until this time.'

Tom drew her to him and kissed her mouth gently, his hands still around her slender waist. 'I know what big girls are like,' he told her with a wry smile, 'and I wish that strong, silent cousin of yours had stayed in Canada.'

Carla lifted her arms and rested them on his shoulders, while she clasped her hands behind his head. 'So do I,' she assured him fervently, and believed she meant it.

Colin had come with a message that old Annie was feeling a little low and if Carla could spare the time later on, would she come and see her for a while, and try to cheer her up. It was the kind of invitation it was hard to resist in any case, and the thought that she might catch a glimpse of Alex's mysterious blonde made it irresistible. She left Tom busy doing something in the outhouses and made her way around the loch to the Carse; a walk she had taken countless times in the past but never failed to enjoy.

The waters of the loch were dark and deep, and the stretch of stony ground that bordered it soon disappeared into the peat-brown wash that the wind raised. Tom declared it smelled foul, but to Carla it smelled only of peat and a damp woody scent from the scrub that leaned over the loch to look at its own reflection and every so often broke off and fell in. It was a rich, earthy smell that she was familiar with, and she pitied Tom for not being able to recognise it and appreciate it as she did.

Over on the far side the patched red and white mass of Alex's Hereford cattle shifted endlessly, but fitted into the scene very neatly, she had to admit. Fruit bushes grew close to the house, and a herb garden, divided from the orderly rows of vegetables by a narrow turf path, while taller fruit trees provided not only a background but also a wind-break. The whole thing flourished under old Annie's keen eye, and Carla felt a tinge of envy for its lush fertility.

The quiet, too, was something she relished, and it was because the normal tranquillity was disturbed by alien sounds today that she frowned as she took the path past the paddock. Apple trees hid the source of the disturbance from her until she had walked a good three-quarters of the distance, but when she saw the reason for it she had difficulty in stifling a desire to laugh. Although it was doubtful if the main participant was finding it very amusing at the moment.

There was a wide space, not really a driveway, in front of the house, and a woman was evidently trying to gain access to the four steps that led up to the front door. Carla had little doubt that she was the same woman Tom had seen in Alex's car, and for a second or two at least her interest was in taking note of the woman rather than the minor drama that was taking place on the front path.

Tall and stunningly blonde, she was wearing dark blue trousers and a paler blue shirt, both expensively tailored to fit an athletically lean figure. A blue and white patterned scarf tied around her throat with its ends floating free added a more feminine touch, and she was very obviously angry as well as frightened; it showed in the jerkiness of her movements.

Bent almost double, she was trying unsuccessfully to shoo away a huge strutting rooster that was doing its best to bar her way to the front door. It made short darting runs at her legs, neck stretched out and wings beating the air menacingly, each sortie accompanied by a screeching squawk that would have seen off the most determined intruder.

The fact that its present victim was a guest and not an intruder was not something it could distinguish at the moment, apparently, and the woman's flapping gestures served only to incite the bird to further aggression. She went on shooing and waving her hands, while she called the creature a variety of uncomplimentary names, some of which came rather strangely from someone who looked so elegantly ladylike, and Carla once more stifled an inclination to laugh.

It wasn't until she got very much closer to the contestants that she spotted Colin standing at the corner of the house, just out of sight of the woman. He was doing absolutely nothing to help her and his faintly malicious smile as he watched the uneven contest surprised Carla. It wasn't like Colin to be spiteful, but he evidently did not share his father's taste in friends.

Carla knew the bird of old, although it was doubtful if it would remember her after all this time. It had been a pet of Colin's since it was a tiny chick, and had long ago taken on the role of guard-dog whenever its meanderings took it round to the front of the house. It was harmless as far as she knew, although its present aggressive attitude scarcely suggested it, and if Colin wasn't going to do anything about making it behave, Carla was. She called out to the creature as she walked across the patch of open ground, making a show of confidence she did not feel; remembering instinctively the name it was known by.

'Cockie! Cockie, come here! Good boy, come here!'

At the sound of her voice three pairs of eyes were turned on her: Colin's, at first startled and then vaguely defiant, the rooster's beady and inquisitive ones and the blue and frankly suspicious ones of the blonde woman. Becoming the centre of attraction suddenly, Carla felt bound to act, and she made straight for the bird who now stood clucking tetchily and undecided what to do next.

She had seen Colin gather it up on more than one occasion and hold it quite easily, and she attempted to do the same, although she was vaguely aware of Colin calling out something as she did so. Bending swiftly, she clapped both hands over the surprised rooster's powerful wings and lifted him off the ground.

But if the bird was prepared to allow such liberties by his master, it was definitely not of the same mind where a virtual stranger was concerned. With an ear-piercing squawk of protest it struggled and managed to get one wing free, then lashed out with its vicious beak at the hand that still held it. With a cry of pain Carla released her hold and dropped the bird to the ground where it shook its rainbow plumage indignantly before stalking off towards the corner where Colin waited to capture it.

But Carla's cry of pain was followed almost immediately by the hysterical shrieks of the blonde woman when she noticed the blood that poured from a gash in Carla's hand. Dazed and not yet fully aware of what was going on around her, Carla felt a surge of relief at the sight of Alex coming swiftly round the corner of the house, and she stared in confusion when, instead of coming to her, as she expected, he went to the woman who stood screaming loudly and shaking her head.

'It could have injured me!' she wailed. 'I could have been torn to shreds with that beak! It's savage, dangerous, it should be put down! It could have injured me!'

Alex seemed not to have noticed Carla yet, standing to one side and holding her injured hand tightly in the other, and she watched him take the other woman by her shoulders and shake her, none too gently. It was Colin who brought the true situation to his notice when, having got rid of the rooster round the other side of the house, he came hurrying over to Carla.

'It's Carla who's hurt, not you!' he told their guest with evident disgust. 'I don't know what *you're* having hysterics about!'

Turning swiftly, Alex saw the truth in a glance and came across to her at once, swearing softly to himself. 'What on earth's been going on out here?' he demanded. 'How the devil did this happen, Carla?'

It was strange, Carla thought, but she felt suddenly very lightheaded, and the realisation that she was going to faint came to her just as Alex took her injured hand in his long fingers and bent over her to look at the wound. Whatever happened next, she knew nothing about. She had a vague impression of Colin gabbling anxiously and of a woman's voice protesting, but what made most impression before she actually became unconscious was the sensation of being lifted in strong arms and held tightly, while a steady, hard beat pounded under the warmth against her cheek.

When she opened her eyes again it was to see old Annie Hepburn's face bent over her, and it was Annie's voice that called her back to consciousness. 'Carla!

Carla—wheesht, lassie, open your eyes, you're all right!'

Then Alex's face drifted into view behind the old lady's left shoulder and Carla noticed he was frowning anxiously, even while anger still lurked in the depth of his brown eyes. Her hand hurt, and she glanced down at the sizeable gash between thumb and forefinger, only the two ends of the wound visible beneath a pad made by a man's handkerchief. Alex's rough and ready first aid, she guessed, and glanced up at him again.

'You'll need to have an anti-tetanus jab,' he told her, and something in his voice made Carla suspect he saw the necessity of taking her to Gibbert hospital for the required injection as a waste of valuable time.

With that in mind, she spoke up quickly. 'Tom will take me!'

Her voice was much more shaky than she antici- pated, and she caught the brief dark frown he gave her as he came to stand where his grandmother had been, right beside the old-fashioned chaise-longue. He looked down at her while she sat herself upright and put her feet to the floor, lending a hand automatically.

'There's no need,' he insisted. 'The accident was our fault, and anyway your friend wouldn't know where the hospital was, and it would take longer.' Reaching down for her hand he moved the handkerchief and examined the wound critically for a moment. 'It's deep,' he said. 'As soon as Colin brings the first-aid box I'll clean it up and put a proper dressing on it.'

For a moment it looked as if old Annie was going to claim the chore for herself, but her bright old eyes darted from Carla to her grandson's stern-looking face and she nodded. 'Aye, you've the steadiest hands, I daresay,' she agreed, then cast her gaze in the direction of the blonde woman who hovered unhappily at the edge of the group; disliking the situation, and doing her best to stay detached from it. Old Annie smiled at her. 'Mebbe to save me, you'd fetch a bowl of water from the kitchen, Caroline?' she suggested. 'There'll be a deal of blood to clean up when Alex starts his doctoring.'

Carla saw the way the smooth cheeks blanched and for a moment it looked as if she too might faint, but she swallowed hard and nodded, making for the kitchen with thankful haste. Caroline and old Annie, Carla suspected, were practised antagonists and for a moment she actually felt sorry for the woman, whoever she was. Annie Hepburn made a good friend, but she could be an implacable enemy and clearly she was not en-amoured of her grandson's woman friend; for Carla was prepared to gamble on it that she had known all about that weakness at the sight of blood.

The water was brought, but not even to stay near Alex would the woman watch him tend Carla's hand. Instead she stood well back, frowning and helpless to do anything about his attention being fully occupied for the moment with Carla. Maybe it was a revelation to her too, the fact that those big, outdoors hands could be so incredibly gentle as they bathed and soothed her wound. And he seemed to recall suddenly that he had not introduced them, remedying the omis-sion without for a second being distracted from what he was doing.

'You've not met Carla before, have you, Caroline? Carla Francis from Hepburn's Quay; Uncle Fergus's granddaughter. You remember I've spoken of him? Carla, this is Caroline Millar.'

He did not, Carla noticed, give her any special status and his manner towards her was rather more that of friendship than romance, yet Annie had men-tioned—— She shrugged off her speculations and mur-mured a polite acknowledgment, her own lack of

warmth drawing an even less enthusiastic response.
Caroline Millar merely inclined her blonde head and
briefly lowered artificially dark lashes as she did so.

'I don't see why Miss Francis can't be taken to the
hospital by—whoever she said,' she told Alex. 'Don't
you think it would be better, Alex, if——'

'No, I don't,' Alex informed her shortly. 'As I said,
this business was our responsibility and I'm unlikely to
lose my way to the hospital like a stranger might. A
gash like this could prove very nasty and the jab should
be given as soon as possible. While we're on the subject,' he added, glancing up at his son, 'I'll have to
consider doing something about that damned rooster
if he can't distinguish between who's allowed in and
who isn't.'

'Oh no, Alex!'

Carla had seen the look on Colin's face and it was
too awful to contemplate him losing his pet because
she had been foolish enough to take a chance. It did
not occur to her for a moment that Alex might be more
concerned with Caroline Millar being attacked again.

But the other woman's eyes showed no such compassion, and they gleamed maliciously. Carla suspected it
was the memory of her humiliating display of hysterics
that made her so determined to have revenge, but even
so, she need not have been quite so insistent. 'Someone
should wring its neck!' she declared, heedless of Colin's
agonised expression. And she darted Carla a narrow-
eyed look of contempt when she again spoke up on the
rooster's behalf.

'Alex, you can't kill him because of this,' Carla
pleaded. She watched his face while he concentrated
on what he was doing and found it impossible to tell
what was going on behind its stern, intent look. 'Cockie
thinks he's protecting his property, you know that; he
isn't normally vicious, and he's Colin's pet—you can't

wring his neck just because he stepped out of line this one time and I was fool enough to try and pick him up.'

'D'ye think mebbe I should wring *your* neck instead?' he asked, and raised his eyes for just a moment. He was close enough for her to see the gleam in their depths, and for her to notice that there were fine lines etched at the corners of them, drawn there by years of squinting long distances against the sun. It was an earthy, outdoor face, strong and confident and so unmistakably masculine that her very feminine senses responded to an alarming degree. Then his mouth eased into a faint smile as he smoothed down the edges of the plaster dressing with his fingertips, speaking so quietly that it was almost as if he intended no one but her to hear what he said. 'I was thinking more of penning the damned thing than wringing its neck.'

'Oh, Alex, I'm glad!'

Carla could not imagine why she felt so suddenly elated, because her hand was if anything more painful than ever after his ministrations. But she looked up at him and smiled with her eyes as well as her mouth, her cheeks slightly flushed and her lips parted. She blinked in surprise when he turned from her abruptly, and her own fingers absently touched the lingering warmth of his on her skin.

'You sit there while I fetch the car round,' he said. 'The sooner you have that jab the better!'

But Caroline Millar was not happy about the arrangement still, and she called him to a halt just as he opened the door to go. 'Can I come too, Alex?' He turned and for a moment regarded her with slightly narrowed eyes. It was a distinctly discouraging look, and the way she angled her chin suggested that she was not used to being discouraged. 'I could keep you company,' she told him, smoothing a hand over her blonde hair in a way that gave added meaning to the words.

'You wouldn't *mind* taking me, surely, Alex?'

'It's not a pleasure trip,' Alex reminded her. 'It'll probably mean waiting around for ages in the waiting-room, and you know how you are about anything to do with hospitals, Caro. I'll run Carla over there, wait till she's had her jab, then get back here as soon as I can, O.K.?'

She did not reply, merely shrugged her shoulders, but Carla had put her own interpretation on his explanation and she thought he saw the whole thing as simply a tedious chore, necessary because his son's pet had been responsible for her being hurt. And she did not want him doing anything for her that he did not do willingly and without making apologies to his woman friend for it.

'Let Tom drive me in, Alex,' she told him. 'You're under no obligation, you know. It was my own fault it happened and I know you'd rather stay here with—I know you'd rather not go.'

'You know nothing of the sort,' Alex informed her with a faint smile, and managed to sound as if he was soothing a fractious child. 'You just stay there. little cousin, I'll be back in a couple of minutes to collect you.'

'Please, Alex!' His manner made her sharply insistent, and he swung back again, startled, she realised, by her vehemence. 'I have to let Tom know I'm going, and he might just as well take me in that case.' Alex was frowning, and his straight mouth showed no hint of a smile. 'I'd *rather* Tom took me, and saved you the——'

'Will you just for once do something without an argument?' Alex interrupted with a gesture of impatience. 'I've said I'll take you to the hospital and that's what I'll do.' He glowered at her from the doorway and Carla was trying to think why he was so de-

termined not to relinquish a chore she would have
thought he was glad to be rid of. 'You sit tight where
you are, and I'll fetch the car, O.K.?'

Carla nodded, but her bottom lip pursed in reproach, and he went out, closing the door noisily
behind him. Catching a look in Annie's eyes, she
wondered too why the old lady looked so satisfied about
his insistence. The Hepburns were never easy to
understand, even when you were one of them.

To Carla's dismay the doctor in Casualty at the hospital decided that the wound needed stitches, and the
process proved much longer and more painful than she
bargained for. Emerging from the cubicle with her
injured hand suspended in a sling, she found herself on
the brink of tears and impatient with her own weakness. Before they reached the outskirts of Gibbert, on
the way home, she could no longer do anything to
stop them, however hard she tried. Reaction was something she had no control over.

Alex summed up the situation from the corner of his
eye, and at the next public house they got to, he drove
into the car park and pulled up. He got out without a
word and came round to open her door, taking her
arms just above her elbows and drawing her gently out
of the seat and into his arms—a gentle, comforting
embrace that she accepted gratefully for the few
moments it lasted.

'Poor little Carla,' he murmured against the silky
softness of her hair. 'Does it hurt a lot, hein? Never
mind, we'll get a wee dram of good Scotch down you
and you'll feel better. Come on.'

She obeyed silently, turning in the curve of his arm
and walking into the quiet little public bar with him.
There were few customers at that hour of the day, and
Alex sat her at a small table in a shadowy corner of the

room while he went off to get her a whisky. It did not even occur to her to deny the need for any kind of reviver, and Colin had been entrusted with the job of telling Tom where she was, so she had no need to fear that he was wondering why she was so long gone.

Alex put the glass down on the table in front of her and gave her a brief encouraging smile before he took a drink from his own glass. 'Are you a hard drinker?' he asked, and made it clear he knew the answer by not waiting for one. 'Then take wee sips, don't drink it straight down.'

In fact the warning was unnecessary, for Carla had no liking for whisky, though she did not tell Alex so, but took a cautious sip, as he said. Looking up, she caught his eye on her, and for some reason she was at a loss to understand, she coloured furiously and hastily looked away again, taking a longer drink to cover her confusion.

'Gently does it, hein!' Alex warned when she gasped for breath as the fiery liquid poured down her throat. 'I don't want to have to take you back there with a choking fit.'

'I'm all right.' She sat clasping her glass tightly between her hands and gazing out of the window rather than look at him again. Lifting her injured hand, she smiled faintly. 'This seems an awful lot of fuss to make for a mere peck from a bird. I feel rather a fraud.'

'Nothing of the sort,' Alex denied. 'I don't believe in taking chances.' He took another sip from his glass, then looked across at her quizzically for a moment before he went on. 'Whatever possessed you to tackle that stupid cockerel the way you did, Carla? Were you trying to show off?'

'Show off?' It hadn't occurred to her until now, but she supposed her action had been a form of showing off. A gesture to let Caroline Millar see that she was

more at home at Hepburn's Carse than she was; and
because she now realised it, she was reluctant to say so.
'Why on earth would I show off, as you call it? I could
see that your—friend was simply making matters worse
by flapping her hands about and shouting, so I grabbed
Cockie the way I've seen Colin do, and tried to get him
out of her way.'

She had used that significant pause for the same
effect he had when he spoke to her about Tom, and she
saw the way his mouth twitched for a moment. Though
it was difficult to tell whether it denoted amusement or
annoyance. 'Caroline is a complete ignoramus about
anything to do with the country, like your Tom,' he
countered after a second or two, 'but you surely know
enough about the farmyard to know what damage an
irate rooster can do. You've spent enough time around
the Carse to have learned that much.'

'*I* see!' Her eyes, still slightly puffy from weeping,
blazed at him angrily across the little table. She had
never resented anything so much in her life as she did
his blaming her in the same breath as he exonerated
Caroline Millar. 'Well, since you think it was my own
fault I got hurt, I'm surprised you insisted on taking
me to hospital yourself instead of letting me go with
Tom, as I wanted to!' She gulped down the rest of the
whisky in her glass so quickly that it left her gasping
for breath, and gave a rasping harshness to her voice
when she carried on with what she had to say without
waiting to recover properly. 'Speaking of Tom, I'd
better be getting back or he'll be worrying about me,
and I'm sure Miss Millar will be livid if *you're* gone
too long. Especially as you promised her you'd get the
unpleasant chore over and done with and get back to
her as soon as possible! Let's go, shall we?'

Ignoring her temper, Alex took another leisurely
drink while he watched her with undisguised amuse-

ment mingled with exasperation. 'What's the matter, hein?' he asked softly. 'Are you jealous?'

Carla stared at him. Her heart was thudding hard and making her alarmingly breathless, but it was her own anger that puzzled her most. She refused to admit that she was jealous of Caroline Millar, no matter how reason warned her that it was the cause of her present agitation. Taking a firm hold on her emotions, she gazed down into the empty glass she held so tightly, and schooled her voice to sound cool, even offhand.

'I don't see where you get that idea from,' she told him. 'If you were talking about Tom, and he and Miss Millar had met, I could see your point, but not otherwise.'

'You're serious about him, then?'

Resentment stirred once more and she tossed back the hair that fell across her brow with a gesture that was unmistakably defiant. 'Are you serious about Miss Millar?' she challenged, and Alex narrowed his brown eyes briefly before he tossed down the last of his whisky.

'Mebbe we'd better get back,' he said, 'before this develops into a slanging match and we both say things we'll be sorry for.' He got to his feet and his strong fingers curled about her upper arm when she pushed back her chair. Slightly dizzy for a moment from the effect of unaccustomed alcohol on top of everything else that had happened, Carla swayed for a moment as she stood up, and immediately he grasped her other arm too, looking down at her, anxiously she thought. 'All right?' he asked, and she nodded.

'Perfectly, thanks!'

The temptation to rest her head on that broad inviting chest and let him hold her until she felt more steady was almost irresistible, but she was determined to resist any such weakness from now on. Looking up, she met his eyes for a second, then almost immediately looked away again.

'Are we going or not?' she asked.

Alex's grip on her tightened until she barely controlled a cry of protest, then he shook his head quickly and turned her towards the door, making her keep pace with his own long, impatient stride. 'We're going,' he told her as they emerged once more into the sunshine, and briefly his brown eyes glowered down at her. 'We'd better before I lose my temper and do something I'll be sorry for!'

CHAPTER FOUR

CARLA found that her hand was much more painful than she expected. It seemed incredible that a bird could inflict such a wound, until she remembered how viciously two cock birds would fight one another, and what awful injuries they could inflict on one another. And Cockie was a big powerful bird, spoiled by over-indulgence and indignant at his loss of dignity.

Although she was far from helpless, it was a relief when another candidate for the post of cleaning woman arrived, and Carla took her on at once, without bothering to consult Tom's opinion. 'I need the help,' she told him as they sat drinking coffee together while the cleaning woman returned to her chores. 'Especially now I have to contend with this wretched hand.'

'Poor darling!' He had not been pleased at her going off to the hospital with Alex, but Tom never bore a grudge for very long. 'But don't take your treasure on permanently, will you, Carla?'

'No?' She caught something in his expression that warned her of the way things were, and she set her cup down carefully on the kitchen table before looking across at him. 'Why not, Tom?'

He looked up; not shamefaced or apologetic, but sorry for all that, she thought. 'It isn't a good enough proposition, love,' he said, without need to enlarge on his meaning. 'I'm sorry, but the old homestead just isn't worth the outlay. It's too small for one thing, and there's really nothing to justify building an extension, which it would need to make it a viable proposition.

It simply isn't a good enough investment, I'm sorry; I wish it was, for your sake.'

Carla supposed she had been half expecting it, but just the same hearing Tom actually say it made her feel like bursting into tears. There was nothing else she could think of at the moment that she could do with the old house that had known some of the happiest times of her life, and she couldn't bear to part with it.

'I'm sorry, darling, honestly.'

And he was, Carla had to believe it, so she smiled at him, however hard it was to do. 'Yes, I know you are, Tom, but I'm grateful that you even considered it, it was a bit of a pipe-dream really.'

'Of course I considered it, darling. I want to do anything that pleases you.' Except send good money after bad, Carla thought ruefully. He reached across and captured her restless fingers. 'I still want to marry you,' he said. 'I don't feel any differently about *that*.'

But it wasn't something that Carla wanted to even think about at the moment, and she drew back her hand. 'I can't think about anything but the Quay at the moment,' she told him. 'I'm sorry, Tom.'

'You'll get rid of it?' He seemed to have little doubt, and frowned when she shook her head. 'You might as well, Carla, it's a white elephant, however attached to it you are.'

Uncertain and unhappy, Carla went on shaking her head. 'I suppose I might just as well have let Alex have it, but—I don't know.'

Ever practical, Tom considered for a moment, then apparently decided against the idea. 'Better to put it up for auction,' he told her. 'You'd get a much better price than making the kind of deal your granddaddy had in mind; he'd almost certainly cut you down in price and you wouldn't feel like bargaining with him. Much better put it into an auction, darling.'

Always the astute businessman, Carla thought wryly, and it did not for a moment occur to him that she might not sell at all, not even to Alex. 'I don't want to sell,' she insisted. 'I simply don't want to part with it, Tom; not to Alex or anyone else. I thought I could part with it, but I can't—I want to keep it.' She noticed his frown and hurried on, throwing out ideas without a thought for the practicality of them. 'Maybe I could make it into a homely boarding-house.'

'Oh, for God's sake!' Tom declared impatiently. 'Do you seriously see yourself as a boarding-house land-lady? Get rid of the damned place, Carla, and marry me—it's what any girl in her right mind would do!'

And it was, of course, Carla knew it, but she was not in the right frame of mind to be persuaded at the moment. 'I won't sell,' she insisted breathlessly, and Tom shook his head slowly.

'You're stubborn,' he said, 'and I wish I knew how to make you change your mind. You're really stubborn, my girl.'

Which was what Alex had said about her refusal to sell, Carla remembered, and touched a finger to her lips. But he had been much more confident of his ability to change her mind.

Tom had gone in to Gibbert to make a telephone call. He could quite easily have made use of the one at Hepburn's Carse, but he said he preferred to drive to Gibbert rather than do that, and Carla despaired of the stubbornness of men. He and Alex had no real reason for disliking one another, she told herself, and yet it was crystal clear that they had made up their minds to do just that.

Carla had decided not to go with him. For one thing because his main reason for going was to ring his father in London, something to do with the firm's business, and for another because she knew in her heart that everything was about to change drastically for her and she needed some time alone to think things out.

She would have to go away from there, she knew, sooner or later, for her grandfather's legacy was too small to make her completely independent, and there was no work available near enough to make a daily journey worthwhile. She would have to make up her mind and fairly quickly, and at the moment she was far too unsure of what she wanted to do about Hepburn's Quay.

It was a warm day and she decided to go for a walk while she tried to work out her future plans, something she had done countless times in the past in her grandfather's company. Not since she had been here this time, though, for Tom was not an enthusiastic walker, and much preferred to go everywhere by car.

She took one of the paths across the carse, making for the hills; the hills that never seemed to become any closer no matter how long you walked. They sat beatifically tranquil on the skyline, luring her on as she made her way over the springy heather, her mind on other walks, other times like this, when the sun was warm and a light wind cooled her cheeks and lifted her hair from her neck and brow.

She chose the other side of the loch from where the cattle grazed, for she had a townsman's wariness of the beasts, on a path that meandered for miles. Most of what she could see in front of her was still Hepburn land, but it was too coarse for good pasture and the cattle were never grazed there, although their soft lowing followed her for quite a distance, for sound travelled far on that still clear air.

It was some time later when she noticed another figure on the expansive spread of the moor, and she narrowed her eyes to try and identify whoever it was.

Not Alex certainly, he would either be on horseback or
in the Land-Rover, but the solitary walker was almost
certainly a Hepburn with that thatch of reddish hair,
and she smiled when she recognised Colin.

He was coming towards her and off a little to her
right, and he seemed to spot her at the same moment
she did him, for he raised an arm and waved, then
started across diagonally, with the obvious intention of
meeting up with her. That pleased her, because Colin
had a curiously reticent air that could so easily be mis-
understood, and yet for some reason he had always
seemed very much at ease with her, although they had
not seen one another very often.

There had been a time when Carla readily admitted
to liking Colin simply because he was Alex's son, but
now that she was older, she recognised him as an individual in his own right. He had a quiet reticence that
made him appear much too mature for his years, but
he was pleasant and friendly to those he liked, and
politely formal to those he didn't. Carla he liked, and
she liked him.

'Hello!' She expelled a breath that stirred the hair
on her forehead, and smiled at him. 'It's much warmer
than I realised when I came out.' He automatically sat
beside her when she sat on a low outcrop of rock that
gave a stunning view across the open carse to the road
she had travelled with Tom, and she looked at him
curiously. 'It seems I'm not the only one given to solo
walking. How far have you been?'

His eyes seemed curiously evasive, and Carla tried to
guess the reason for it, and for that oddly defensive
expression he wore. 'I've been visiting,' he told her.
Then, seeing her frown at the seemingly empty moor,
he pointed out a dip in the ground, some distance away
and roughed around with the bristly darkness of
heather. 'There's a croft in the dip there.'

'A croft?'

It surprised her, for she had never heard of Hepburn's Carse having tenants. But Colin was shaking his head, his lower lip thrust out slightly. 'Not on Alex's land,' he said. 'Just beyond it.'

That reference to his father had sounded so bleak and unfriendly, and Carla noticed how he referred to the carse as his father's land instead of using a more possessive pronoun as might be expected. She noticed too how he now called Alex by his christian name rather than the more affectionate Dadda he had used as a child. Obviously old Annie had been right about him resenting his father's return, but she wondered how Alex felt about it.

She shook her head, coming back to the croft he had been visiting, and still more curious to know what he had been doing there. 'I didn't even know it was there,' she told him, 'but then I've never really walked quite that far with Grampy. Have you got some friends who live there? I thought all your school friends lived in Gibbert.'

Colin sat with his thin young hands clasped between his knees, and his eyes were fixed on the distant road into Gibbert. It was always better, she had found, to wait for him to go on rather than to prompt him, and she was in no particular hurry. 'The McKinnons live there,' he said after a moment or two, and hurried on when he saw her politely raised brows. 'My grandparents.'

Light dawned and she smiled. 'Oh yes, of course; your mother was Isabella McKinnon, wasn't she?'

Colin nodded, then sat for a moment or two longer before he spoke again. And it seemed to Carla that he chose his words carefully. 'I wondered—did you ever know her, Carla? Enough to remember what she was like?'

Unsure what he was leading up to, Carla thought before she spoke. She remembered Isabella McKinnon only as a small dark face with the same rather shy and wistful grey eyes that Colin had. As a personality she had made no impression at all, although a child's memory of such things was hardly a reliable yardstick by which to judge.

'I honestly don't remember her very well at all,' she admitted after a moment or two. 'I was only eight years old when she died, remember, and you don't really *know* people at that age, if you know what I mean.'

Colin nodded, as if he knew exactly what she meant. 'Like I didn't really know Alex before he went away,' he said. 'I was only nine and he seemed so—different. I don't know—I just don't seem to remember him the way he is now.'

'He's the same,' Carla assured him quietly, finding the one parent as discomfiting to discuss as the other. 'At least—not different enough to make any odds.' She guessed Colin was not inclined to agree with that in his present state of mind, so she switched the subject back to the McKinnons. At least Isabella McKinnon was not alive to object to her opinion. 'How are your McKinnon grandparents?' she asked.

Colin still kept his eyes on the distant road, but she noticed how his hands clasped more tightly together suddenly before he answered her. 'Well enough,' he replied, and sounded uncannily like an echo of his father when he said it. 'But they're to lose their house.'

'Oh, Colin, no! How awful!' She looked at his serious young face and understood his solemnity on this occasion. 'But how? Why? Can't anything be done to help them?'

'It's been condemned as unfit.' His mouth had a tight angry look that was again much more reminiscent of his father than he probably realised. 'It has to be knocked down, they say, it's old and——' He made a touchingly helpless gesture with his thin hands. 'They've been told they're allocated a council house in Gibbert.'

'Oh well, at least they'll have somewhere to go,' Carla said, relieved for his sake and puzzled by his continued frown. 'They'll be housed, Colin, and that's what counts, isn't it?'

'It's not as good as it sounds first off,' he told her, twirling a twig of dry heather round and round in his fingers while he spoke. 'I know how I'd feel in their place—I'd hate it. They're country people, open-air people, they've never been shut up on a council estate, they've seldom been into town even, and they'll be square pegs in round holes, with pavements instead of the carse around them.'

It was not hard to guess that he was quoting his grandparents' opinion, but she wondered if they had realised when they voiced the complaint just how much they had worried the boy, and she was gentle as she pressed a hand over his in sympathy.

'I'm sorry,' she said softly. 'I can imagine what it will be like for them.'

'If only there was *somewhere*! Somewhere not too far from where they are now.'

She did not for a moment suspect he was trying to force her hand, but something in his desperation kindled her brain into action, although it was a moment or two before the glimmerings of an idea came to her. She had envisaged something very different for Hepburn's Quay, but if Colin's grandparents were looking for somewhere to live, and she had to decide between parting with Hepburn's Quay and finding some way of making it pay its way, maybe this was the answer. Although it would need some thought first, and

she put it cautiously to Colin. 'If they're really desperate——' she began, then hesitated again. 'I mean, I
know how they must feel about leaving the carse to live
in a town, and I might—I just *might* be able to house
them at the Quay.'

His grey eyes turned on her with the startled innocence of a child, and Carla wondered if she could possibly have misconstrued his intention after all. 'Carla,
I didn't mean for you to——'

'No, no, really, I will give it some thought,' she promised, smiling at him reassuringly. 'I suppose you know
that we had plans for turning the Quay into an hotel?'
He nodded. 'Well, it's fallen through. The house just
isn't suitable and we've had to abandon the idea. But
I have to think of something else to do with it.'

'You're not selling it to Alex?' She surely imagined
that hint of malice in his eyes when he asked it, and she
shook her head, though rather less certainly than usual.

'It's going to take a lot of thinking about before I
know *what* to do with it,' she confessed. Getting to her
feet, she looked down at him and smiled invitingly as
she smoothed blue jeans down over her slim hips. 'Can
I come back with you? I can't tackle any more walking
today, I'm out of practice.'

Colin nodded without speaking. He must surely be
very like his mother, she thought, for he did not take
after the garrulous Hepburns. But he willingly stepped
out with her as she walked back towards the loch and
she did not mind in the least that they went in almost
complete silence. Colin probably had a great deal on
his mind, and her grandfather had often said that a
walk like this should only sparingly be scattered with
words, so that one could appreciate the surroundings.

She automatically took the same route that Colin
did, when they came to the dividing paths, and accompanied him to Hepburn's Carse. Though she alone

waved a greeting to Alex who stood over by the paddock fence; Colin merely nodded his head briefly, then turned off and went to the house instead of coming with her to join his father. He was a strange, solitary child, she thought, and wondered just how much blame for it could be laid at Alex's door.

Alex watched him go into the house, and showed no reaction at all on that strong, implacable face of his; but his brown eyes followed him every inch of the way with a curious kind of longing in their depths. When he looked back at her, the impression was gone and he leaned casually against the fence with one arm along the top bar.

He looked so much darker, Carla recognised, when he wore a white shirt. It was open at the neck and showed a deep vee of bronzed throat and chest, revealing a small restless pulse at the base of his throat that gave an unexpected impression of vulnerability. He turned right around when she joined him and together they gazed at the occupants of the paddock.

Neither of them said anything for a moment or two, until Alex turned his head suddenly and looked down at her. His gaze slid down from her face to the slender figure in a shirt and blue jeans, and he raised a brow, his mouth hinting at a smile, 'You're dressed for it,' he said. 'Would you like to ride out with me?'

'I'd love to!' She did not hesitate, nor even stop to think why he had invited her instead of Caroline Millar who, as far as she knew, was still there. A little ripple of laughter recognised and admitted her own impulsiveness, and she pulled a face. 'As long as you've got something not too frisky for me to ride. I haven't been out for ages.'

'You never forget,' Alex promised her briskly, and immediately turned towards the stables, so that she wondered if he could possibly have seen her coming with Colin, and waited to invite her. 'Come away, if you're coming, I'm usually out by now.'

Obediently she followed him to the cluster of buildings, low and white and new since her last visit, at the far end of the paddock. A middle-aged man whom she vaguely recognised gave her a brief, unsmiling nod as they crossed the yard, but Carla was already beginning to wonder if she had been too impulsive in accepting the invitation, for it was a very long time since she rode last.

'Find me something *very* quiet,' she stressed, staying outside while Alex went on into the stable building, and he half-turned his head and cocked a faintly derisive brow at her.

'I've a wee gentle mare here that'd carry a maiden aunt without upsetting her dignity,' he told her. 'You're surely not getting cold feet already, Carla, are you?'

'Frankly, yes!' She caught his eye and angled her chin slightly when she saw the way he looked at her. 'I don't want to be thrown, Alex. I've enough trouble already with this wretched hand; in fact perhaps I'd better not——'

'Och, will you stop havering, woman,' he scolded impatiently. 'You can handle this gentle creature with one hand behind you, and I'm here if you do get into any trouble.'

Carla thought how much she would have given in the old days to have been invited to go riding with Alex. Side by side over the wide, fresh acres of the carse, enjoying the special rapport that such occasions often bring. She would have died of sheer pleasure at seventeen, just to be given the chance, and yet here she was, only six years later, thinking about having second thoughts.

Not that it looked as if she was to be allowed to have

second thoughts, for Alex was already saddling her mount, and she watched him with a kind of excitement stirring in her. He was so deft and sure, so gentle and yet so definitely the man in charge; a curiously contradictory man and an alarmingly disturbing one in any circumstances.

He had selected a small neat bay mare with the proud look of the Arab about her head and beautifully arched neck, who dipped her head submissively to the bridle and responded to the softly murmured words he said to her. She looked perfect for a quiet ride, and Carla took heart once more as Alex led her out into the yard.

Cupping his hands, he looked at Carla with a hint of a frown. 'Up with you,' he said. 'You can get the feel of her while I saddle my own, and you've no need to worry that she'll throw you; she's far too much of a lady for that.'

Obediently Carla put one foot into his cupped palms and clung tight to the saddle while he lifted her easily off the ground. The rest was automatic, and certainly the little mare showed no sign of resenting her passenger; instead she flicked her ears appreciatively when Carla rubbed her neck.

The mount Alex chose for himself was not the big grey stallion he had ridden the last time she saw him on horseback, but another mare. Bigger and broader and much more wilful, although she was well under control when Alex rode across the yard to join Carla. He stroked a soothing hand down the glossy dark neck and gave Carla a half-smile.

'It looks like it's an all-girl outing today,' he told her. 'So just you all remember who's in charge of the party, O.K.? Shall we go?'

They headed out across the carse in the direction of the grazing cattle, now some distance from the loch,

and Alex kept the pace easy, so that she had no cause
for complaint. Not that she wished to complain, for she
had so often dreamed about riding out with Alex like
this, though not perhaps with quite the same feeling of
wariness she had at the moment, lurking somewhere
below the excitement.

The little mare responded nicely, and before they
had gone very far, Carla felt much more at ease and
began to really enjoy herself. The blue hills looked
misty, and she remembered that Grampy had always
said that often meant rain to come, although there
were no other clouds but a few small white ones that
hovered lazily about the tops of the hills. It was perhaps because she was feeling so relaxed and happy that
she thought about Colin again, and how sober and
serious he always was. And it occurred to her that he
could have come with them too.

'Wouldn't Colin have enjoyed this?' she ventured,
watching Alex's face from the corner of her eye.

He raised a brow and cast her a brief, half-concealed
glance. 'He'd not come,' he told her in a flat and matter-
of-fact voice. 'Not with me, though you could mebbe
have tempted him.'

It troubled her; not only that Colin felt as he did
about his father, but that Alex seemed to accept it, and
she shook her head slowly. 'Alex, I'm sure you must be
wrong—about him not coming with you.'

He was smiling, but it wasn't a pleasant smile. It
twisted his firm mouth into a parody of amusement and
there was hurt, not laughter in the brown eyes when
she caught a glimpse of them before he looked away.
'Have you not noticed,' he said, 'that I'm not a riotous
success as a father?'

Carla tried to think what to say to him, but it wasn't
easy to think of anything. It was true, what he said, to
some extent, but it was difficult to apportion blame in

a situation like his and Colin's. For five of the most important years of his life Colin had had to do without his father, and possibly he was entitled in some way to resent his coming home again and trying to resume the role of parent.

But when Alex had gone, it had been with the intention of gaining the necessary know-how and finance to transform Hepburn's Carse into something that any man would be proud to leave to his son. To have made a quite ordinary country estate into something as prosperous as the Carse now was, was quite an achievement, and it seemed hard that he should have lost the affection of the son he had done it for.

'Mebbe it's as well I've only the one, eh?' he asked, but again with no humour in his smile.

He sat easy in the saddle while the mare ambled along in the sunshine, but although the lean body looked relaxed, there were telltale signs that suggested otherwise. His big firm hands held the reins tightly, yet without pulling too hard on the bit, and they were drawn back against a flat, hard stomach instead of resting on the bow of the saddle.

'Unless you get married again.'

Carla noticed how light and breathless her voice sounded, and she had spoken impulsively, without stopping to think, so that she flushed when he turned and regarded her for a moment with steady brown eyes. 'There's always that possibility, I suppose,' he agreed quietly. 'Had you anybody in mind for me, Carla?'

Feeling rather as if she had walked into a trap of her own making, Carla was tempted to put her heels to the mare's flanks and ride off without him. But instead she simply avoided looking at him and tried to keep her voice as steadily matter-of-fact as she could manage.

'What about Miss Millar?'

'Hmm.' It was difficult to believe that amusement lurked in his eyes when she turned her head and looked at him for a second, but his accent was stronger and broader when he went on. 'D'ye see Caroline as the kind of woman who'd want a house full o' bairns, hein? D'ye think she's cut out for a Hepburn wife on my side of the family?'

Realising that he was taunting her with her own rashness in suggesting it, Carla grew angry as well as embarrassed. 'You don't have to follow old Johnnie's example to the letter!' she told him breathlessly, and he took her up immediately, his brown eyes gleaming.

'Why not?' he demanded. 'We always have! My father was the first to have an only child and Grandmother hoped for better things from me!'

Struggling with a conversation that had gone much further than she had ever intended, Carla shook her head. 'I simply meant that if you married again and had other children it would mean you'd have someone else to leave all this to, and Colin could follow his own inclinations and become a vet.'

It was rather puzzling to realise that he was less angry than she would have expected at her taking such an interest in his personal affairs. Instead he was looking at her again, more curious than annoyed. 'You think I'm very hard on him, don't you, Carla?'

'Yes!' If it was not true, it was near enough, and she owed him something for embarrassing her as he had. 'Because I'd rather he benefited from all this instead of spending his days turning out at all hours to give jabs to sick cows?'

He swept one hand round expansively, and she followed his direction, sympathising with him, but seeing Colin's point of view as well. 'If he'd be happier doing it, Alex——'

'And what the devil is there about inheriting a place

like Hepburn's Carse that could make him so unhappy?' he demanded. It must surely have been despair
at his son's stubbornness that made him say what he
did next, for he would never have said it otherwise, she
knew. 'Och, he's too much of a McKinnon to think like
a Hepburn!'

Carla shrank from his harshness, even while she
sympathised with his feelings, but his mentioning the
fact of Colin being part McKinnon gave her an opportunity of turning the subject, and she took it quickly.
'I know he's unhappy at the moment about his grandparents,' she told him, and knew from his look that he
had not heard about the threatened eviction of his in-
laws. 'The McKinnons are being evicted from their
house, apparently. Colin told me it's been condemned.'

'I'm not surprised!' Alex declared harshly, but was
nevertheless not completely unsympathetic, she
guessed. 'The damned place hasn't been fit to house
pigs for the past fifteen years at least!'

At the time when he would have been courting and
marrying Isabella McKinnon, Carla realised, and for
the first time stopped to wonder what kind of a background Colin's mother had come from. 'But it's hard
on them,' she pointed out. 'Especially as the council are
going to rehouse them on a council estate in Gibbert.
Country people in a town setting,' she explained when
he looked at her curiously, then hurried on while the
notion was still in her mind. 'I've been thinking, now
that the hotel idea has fallen through——'

'It has?'

His head turned swiftly, eyes slightly narrowed, and
Carla avoided them. 'Tom is convinced it won't be a
viable proposition, and I have to take his word for it.'

'Will you now sell it to me, then?'

Somehow it was much more difficult to refuse him
now, and Carla still avoided looking at him as she

shook her head slowly. 'No, Alex. I still don't want to part with it—I'm sorry.'

'You likely will be before long!' Alex retorted. 'What *are* you going to do with it?'

She hesitated, then went on, knowing he would dislike any alternative to selling it to him, no matter what it was, 'I thought perhaps I could find room for the McKinnons, in the circumstances.'

'No!'

His flat hard denial made her jump, but when she recovered from her surprise, she frowned at him. 'I don't see why not,' she told him, determined not to be browbeaten. After all, she knew why he objected to her having someone there, paying rent to help her keep the house on. 'Why shouldn't I give them a place when they need one?'

He kept his face forward and did not even glance at her, but she saw the dark, straight line of his brows drawn across his forehead. 'For one thing because they're not——' He looked at her briefly, but not directly into her eyes, and that wasn't like him. 'Have you met them?'

'No, I haven't.'

He was quiet once more; a dark, brooding quietness that made her uneasy. 'What's wrong with them, Alex?' The brooding frown stayed in place, but he cast her a swift glance from the corners of his eyes. 'If they're Colin's grandparents, they must be decent folks, surely?'

They rode through the grazing cattle that moved lazily aside to let them pass, but Carla was so involved in Alex's dark forbidding mood that she barely noticed them, and felt none of her usual apprehension. 'They're a tinker family,' he said, after what seemed like an eternity, and Carla felt her heart lurch sickeningly in her breast as she stared at him.

The travelling tinkers had once been a fairly familiar sight on the lonely moorland roads. Dirty, poor and not above thieving to keep body and soul together, they had been the bane of the country-dweller's life. Things had improved during the past twenty years or so, but there were still some who preferred the bleak, shifty life on the road to living in a croft and doing a regular job.

A lot of those that did settle never really changed in any other way, and living in a permanent habitation did nothing to change their traditional habits. They were still poachers and small-time thieves, and the idea of Alex having found his wife from among such people was too staggering to contemplate for a moment. It gave her a completely new slant on his past, and she wondered how old Annie had felt about his choice of a bride.

'Blane McKinnon has spent more time in the county jail in Gibbert than he has in that hovel he calls home,' Alex went on, apparently bent on making a clean breast of the whole thing now that he had begun. 'He's never done an honest day's work in his life, but he's fathered six children, and Isabella was the oldest of them.' His voice seemed to gentle suddenly when he spoke of her, and for a moment the harsh, trap-like cruelty of his mouth eased slightly. 'God knows how they managed to have a daughter like her. She was as pretty as a doll and sweet and clean too, not filthy like the rest of them. I'd never even been near a tinker before, and I suppose she was so—unexpected that I found her irresistible.'

'You fell in love with her,' Carla guessed, feeling a lump in her throat for the pretty girl who had had so much against her and died so young.

'Love?' Alex looked at her for a moment, his brown eyes deep and unfathomable, then he shook his head. 'I don't think love came into it, but I was—drawn to her; we were like two young animals. I wasn't quite twenty; and she wasn't just pretty, she was a woman even though she was only seventeen. No, I wouldn't call it love, hein.'

Somehow that endearment made his bluntness even more stark, and she took a moment or two to gather her thoughts, trying to come to terms with a much different Alex from the one she had always thought she knew. That he was a passionate man, she had never doubted; all the Hepburns were fiery in temperament, but Alex she had always thought to be ruled by a very strong streak of puritanism in his make-up, and it was finding that was not always so that she had to learn to accept.

'But you married her,' she said, and Alex once more gave her a firm, direct look.

'She claimed to be having my child,' he said in a flat quiet voice. 'Of course I married her.'

'But——' She stared at him wide-eyed for a moment, betraying the fact that she had noticed how he worded that first sentence.

But Alex was shaking his head and his mouth showed another of those strangely twisted smiles. 'Oh, aye, he's Hepburn all right,' he assured her. 'But he wasn't in too much hurry to be born!'

'Oh, Alex!'

She said it softly, and he cocked a derisive brow at her, as if he mocked her sympathy, although she refused to believe he was really that uncaring. 'Grandmother near died to think of the future of the Carse Hepburns being dependent on a tinker's daughter,' he told her with harsh bluntness, 'but she treated Isabella as gently as you'd expect her to, and she actually cried when she died having Colin.'

'Poor girl!'

He gave her a faintly rueful half-smile and nodded his head. 'Aye,' he said, 'she made a bid to escape, and God knows I'm the last one to blame her for that. But she couldn't have known what the result would be, surely.'

It was a surprise to Carla to realise just how far they had ridden. They were already right the other side of the carse, where the river curved around almost into a circle before making for the foothills, and it was by mutual consent that they dismounted to give the horses a short breather.

Where they stood, goat willows clustered close to the water's edge, pale and softly swaying in the fairly brisk wind; hiding both Hepburn's Carse and the Quay from immediate view, and giving the impression of a quiet and solitary little world of their own.

It was a situation she had so often dreamed of before Alex went away, but which was so much different from what she expected, because Alex did not seem quite the same man. At seventeen she had seen him as strong and invincible, not subject to the weaknesses of other men, and now she knew just how wrong that picture of him had been.

He was still a ruggedly attractive man and his essential maleness had increased with maturity. He was if anything even more disturbing, for there was an element of excitement in being with him that her youthful adoration had never allowed her to experience.

Leaning against one of the willows, he looked across at the hills soaring up into the summer sky, and his eyes had a curiously absent look, so that she wondered if he could be thinking about his young wife still. She was not quick enough to avoid his gaze when the brown eyes were turned suddenly in her direction, and he smiled—that slow, warm smile that was rare enough to set her heart clamouring urgently.

'Canada is very like this in places, did you know
that?' he asked, and she nodded, her eyes shifting uneasily from his scrutiny.

'Yes, I've heard it is. You liked it there, didn't you,
Alex?'

His gaze shifted, scanning the carse with its fertile
pastures and the bright water of the river snaking
across its greenness, and he smiled acknowledgment.
'I liked it fine,' he admitted, 'but I was glad to come
home. And now that I've been back for a little over a
year it's as if I was never away from it.'

It was as if she had glimpsed right into his heart for
a moment, and Carla spoke softly and with a slightly
breathless sound to her voice. 'You love it, of course,
it's your home; it's where you belong.'

She had his full attention again. Easing himself away
from the supporting tree, he came and stood close beside her, one hand resting on the slim willow trunk
behind her and his arm stretched out, just lightly
touching her if she turned her head. He was much too
close for comfort, and all the wild longings of that
much younger Carla sprang into being again, and made
her fight to resist leaning back against the warmth that
his nearness promised.

'It's where all the Hepburns belong,' he said, and his
words stirred the hair on the top of her head, making
her shiver suddenly.

'Except me, surely?' she suggested with an unsteady
ripple of laughter. 'You can't think I belong here or
you wouldn't be so anxious for me to sell you the Quay
and get out.'

'I'm anxious for you to sell me the Quay, I admit.'
His voice again stirred the strands of hair on her crown,
and the arm behind her descended gently to rest on her
shoulders, strong fingers curving into her soft upper

Get your
Harlequin Romance
Home Subscription NOW!

and get these 4 best-selling novels FREE!

Harlequin Romance
Teachers Must Learn
NERINA HILLIARD

Harlequin Romance
Cap Flamingo
VIOLET WINSPEAR

Harlequin Romance
THE Arrogant Duke
ANNE MATHER

Harlequin Romance
Beyond the Sweet Waters
ANNE HAMPSON

If you were in their place what would you do?

Jeanette...

Though she has survived a heart-wrenching tragedy, is there more unhappiness in store for Jeanette? She is hopelessly in love with a man who is inaccessible to her. Her story will come alive in the pages of "Beyond the Sweet Waters" by Anne Hampson.

Juliet...

Rather than let her father choose her husband, she ran...ran into the life of the haughty duke and his intriguing household on a Caribbean island. It's an intimate story that will stir you as you read "The Arrogant Duke" by Anne Mather.

Laurel...

There was no turning back for Laurel. She was playing out a charade with the arrogant plantation owner, and the stakes were "love". It's all part of a thrilling romantic adventure called "Teachers Must Learn" by Nerina Hilliard.

Fern...

She tried to escape to a new life...a new world...now she was faced with a loveless marriage of convenience. How long could she wait for the love she so strongly craved to come to her...Live with Fern...love with Fern...in the exciting "Cap Flamingo" by Violet Winspear.

Jeanette, Juliet, Laurel, Fern...these are some of the memorable people who come alive in the pages of Harlequin Romance novels. And now, without leaving your home, you can share their most intimate moments!

It's the easiest and most convenient way to get every one of the exciting Harlequin Romance novels! And now, with a home subscription plan you won't miss *any* of these true-to-life stories, and you don't even have to go out looking for them.

You pay nothing extra for this convenience, there are no additional charges ...and you don't even pay for postage!

Fill out and send us the handy coupon now, and we'll send you 4 exciting Harlequin Romance novels absolutely FREE!

A Home Subscription! It's the easiest and most convenient way to get every one of the exciting Harlequin Romance Novels!

...and you'll get 4 of them FREE

$5.00 GIFT TOKEN

Yes,

I'd like to take advantage of the Harlequin Reader Service offer.

Send no money get these

four books FREE

Mail this card today to:

Harlequin Reader Service
901 Fuhrmann Blvd., Buffalo, N.Y. 14203

YES, please start a *Harlequin Romance* home subscription in my name, and send me FREE and without obligation my 4 *Harlequin Romances*. If you do not hear from me after I have examined my 4 FREE books, please send me the 6 new *Harlequin Romances* each month as soon as they come off the presses. I understand that I will be billed only $1.25 per book (total $7.50). There are no shipping and handling nor any other hidden charges. There is no minimum number of books that I have to purchase. In fact, I can cancel this arrangement at any time. The first 4 books are mine to keep as a FREE gift, even if I do not buy any additional books.

CR952

NAME

ADDRESS

CITY   STATE   ZIP CODE

This offer expires Oct. 31, 1980. Prices subject to change without notice.
Offer not valid to present subscribers.

Get your
Harlequin Romance
Home Subscription NOW!

- ● Never miss a title! ● Get them first—straight from the presses! ● No additional costs for home delivery!
- ● These first 4 novels are yours—FREE!

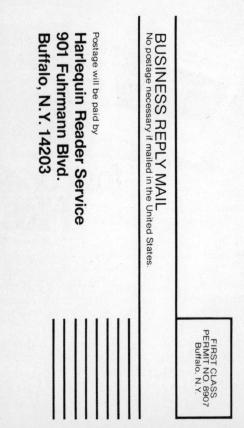

For exciting details, see special offer inside.

Printed in U.S.A.

BUSINESS REPLY MAIL
No postage necessary if mailed in the United States.

Postage will be paid by

Harlequin Reader Service
901 Fuhrmann Blvd.
Buffalo, N.Y. 14203

FIRST CLASS
PERMIT NO. 8907
Buffalo, N.Y.

arm. 'But I'm not so anxious to see you go, Carla. How can you think it?'

'Because it's the only way you see yourself getting what you want.' Her limbs trembled and she leaned quite instinctively against him, supported by that encircling arm. 'I know you,' she told him in a shiveringly small voice. 'You want Hepburn's Quay, Alex, and you're not used to doing without anything you've set your mind on—you're a Hepburn through and through!'

'That I am!' he agreed without hesitation.

Turning her towards him within the circle of his arm, he drew her against the lean, vigorous length of him, holding her tightly with both arms while he looked down into her face. Brown eyes gleamed darkly between their thick lashes and further weakened a resistance that was already only half-hearted. She remembered the touch of his mouth from that brief kiss he had once given her on parting, but she was not prepared for the almost brutal fierceness that parted her lips and seemed to draw the very breath from her body.

It was like dying and being reborn all in one stunning moment, and while her body clamoured for relief from the assault, her senses longed for it to go on for ever. Big, gentle hands soothed her while his mouth possessed and ravished, and refused to give up possession even when she fought for breath. She clung to him tightly until she felt herself slipping into a kind of breathless oblivion, and only then did she try to free herself.

Shaken and trembling, she broke away, her face turned from him as she moved to the very edge of the water, as if the sight of its chilling greyness could cool the fiery glow that burned in her. Never in her wildest dreams had she imagined he would kiss her like that, and she was so shaken by her own response to him that she sought for reasons why he had done so, without even admitting the most obvious one.

He said nothing, but seemed to be waiting for her to break the brittle silence, and she half-turned her head like a startled fawn when she caught a faint sound of movement; green eyes bright and shining between their lashes. It was hard to tell, but she thought his mouth curved into a smile before she turned back again to stare into the deep grey-brown waters of the river.

'I'll not touch you again, Carla,' he said, and the very timbre of his voice made her shiver with that same thrill of excitement. 'I promise you'll have nothing to explain to your—friend.'

Illogically perhaps, she took exception to that slight pause, as she had done on other occasions, but she had not the necessary self-possession in this instance to say so. Instead she tried hard to give her words a ring of confidence, even though she said them without turning round. 'I don't have to explain anything to Tom,' she said. 'But you won't influence me to let you have Hepburn's Quay like that, you know.'

A long finger traced a shivering line down the centre of her back, and she felt herself stiffen against the expected touch of his body. But instead he reached for her hand and turned her round until she stood beside him. 'I'm entitled to try,' he said quietly, and when she turned on him like an angry cat, he tightened his grip on her hand and looked down at her with dark gleaming eyes. 'Shall we ride back?' he suggested.

CHAPTER FIVE

ALL too frequently during the next couple of days, Carla looked for Alex coming. He didn't come, but Colin brought the welcome news that the McKinnons were to be rehoused not in a council house after all, but in a cottage about four miles away.

From his manner, Carla realised for the first time that his concern for his maternal grandparents stemmed more from a sense of duty than from any affection he had for them. He was pleased for their sake that they had somewhere, but relieved for his own that it was further away, she gathered. And Carla had to admit it was a weight off her own mind.

She did not know what she would have done if she had made a more firm offer to Colin about having them at Hepburn's Quay, and they had taken her up on it. After what Alex had told her about his in-laws she could see how impossible the situation would have been. It had been a narrow escape, and she thanked heaven for Alex's unexpected frankness.

Now that he was firmly decided against the hotel, Tom was impatient to get back to London, but he was unwilling to go without Carla, and she had still to make up her mind. He sat watching her while she prepared the vegetables for their dinner, and a frown marred his normally good-natured face.

'You don't look right in the domestic role, darling,' he told her. 'I much prefer you in high heels and snazzy little office outfits than the pinny and the paring knife.' He leaned across the table and smiled up at her, resting his chin on one hand as he did so. 'Will you marry me, Carla?'

It was a subject that Carla avoided if she possibly could. She had done her very best to be discouraging without being unkind, but Tom was not easily put off, and she had half-expected this new proposal. Nevertheless she steadfastly refused to meet his eyes, however hard he tried to make her. 'I'm sorry, Tom. I've told you——'

'I know what you've *told* me, sweetheart,' he interrupted cheerfully, 'but I'm getting desperate.' The way he was smiling at her would, she imagined, have coaxed any girl who was not firmly convinced she could never fall in love with him. 'Pop's over the moon because I've at last found somebody I actually want to marry and settle down with. He's really chuffed about it.'

'Doesn't he mind that it's your secretary that you want to marry?' Carla asked, and Tom grinned.

'*Ex*-secretary,' he reminded her. 'You gave me notice, remember?'

Carla gave him a brief glance from below her lashes, but went on with what she was doing. 'I'm still an ex-employee,' she pointed out. 'I'm sure he had somebody different in mind for his son and heir, Tom.'

'Not Pop,' Tom assured her quickly. 'He's not a bit class-conscious.'

But Mrs Laxey was, Carla remembered, and she looked at Tom directly for a moment while she confirmed it. 'What about your mother?' she asked. 'I seem to remember she wasn't very pleased when you started asking me out.'

'Oh, Ma!'

He shrugged carelessly, but Carla knew that his autocratic and formidable mother would have been a very real stumbling block if she had been inclined to accept. With that in mind she thanked heaven that all she felt for Tom was a warm friendliness that had no likelihood of ever developing into anything more serious.

She did not consider she had given him a false impression by letting him drive her up to Hepburn's Quay, because she had genuinely believed that the hotel idea was a sound one. And Tom had been glad to give her his opinion and his promise of possible investment.

'I'm sorry, Tom, but I really mean it.' She stopped what she was doing for a moment to give stress to her insistence. 'I'm quite definite about it, and I shan't change my mind whatever you say or do.'

For a moment he sat gazing at a spot just beyond her, while she went back to preparing their dinner, and Carla felt more sorry about it than she had ever done about anything in her life. She liked Tom, and that was all, but she hated having to sound so brutally final about turning him down.

Tom being Tom, however, his recovery was quick, at least superficially it was, and he smiled across at her ruefully. 'In other words,' he said, 'I might as well pack my bags and go back to the smoke. Well, I shan't—not just yet.' She looked up for a moment, frowning, and he sought to disarm her with another smile. 'I shall hang around for a week or two, darling, in the hope of taking you back with me.'

'But I might not *go* back,' she warned.

'I shall hang about in the hope that I can do something to help you make up your mind,' Tom told her. 'I'm a very decisive type, love, and I think you need a little shove occasionally to help you decide.'

'Maybe.' She admitted it reluctantly. 'I had thoughts of giving rooms to the McKinnons—you know, Colin's other grandparents, but that won't be necessary now. Still, I——'

'Phew, thank goodness for that!' Tom made a show of mopping his brow and he was so obviously relieved to hear about the McKinnons that Carla eyed him suspiciously. She knew he had been up to something when he leaned across the table and took one of her hands in his, but she could not imagine what it might be. 'You couldn't sell it once you'd got tenants in,' he said.

'I don't want to sell it, Tom, that's the whole idea. That's why I wouldn't let Alex have it, like he says Grampy agreed to.' She freed her hand, but she was still vaguely suspicious. 'I've got a sentimental attachment for the Quay, Tom, you know that.'

'You should learn,' Tom told her with a hint of rebuke, 'that sentiment has no place in business.' He folded his arms on the table and once more that slightly mysterious smile niggled at her suspicions. 'Except of course when you fall in love with your beautiful secretary, like I did.'

Carla stirred uneasily under his bemused gaze. 'Tom, I——'

'I know, I know,' he interrupted softly. 'But all's fair in love, my angel, and the way I see it is that as long as I go on hanging about and giving you a little shove in the right direction occasionally, you may eventually see things my way.'

She smiled in spite of herself. 'What kind of a shove?'

His hands spread, Tom winked an eye and looked rather too pleased with himself. 'Oh—just a gentle nudge,' he said. 'I'm a great believer in happy endings, love.'

Carla thought about Isabella McKinnon's try at making her own happy ending; a gamble on making a better future, that she had never lived long enough to enjoy. And she thought about her own youthful dreams about Alex. Smiling ruefully at Tom, she shook her head and got on with what she was doing.

'Aren't we all?' she said.

It was always a good excuse for visiting Hepburn's

Carse when they needed eggs or milk and butter, and
Carla always enjoyed going. She liked to see Annie, but
in this instance she frankly admitted, at least to herself, that her main interest was in seeing Alex again.
Even though he had more or less told her that the kiss
that had affected her so deeply was an attempt to per-
suade her to part with Hepburn's Quay.

Whether or not his objective had been to get what
he wanted, she had always dreamed of being kissed in
the way he had kissed her. And she repeatedly told herself that she had always known Alex was a man who
knew how to get what he wanted, so that she made
excuses for him rather than for herself. She had refused
to sell Hepburn's Quay to him and he had declared
himself capable of persuading her to change her mind,
so that she should have expected something of the kind
to happen. But whatever his motive, his kiss had
aroused a whole gamut of new emotions, and left her
with an irresistible desire to see him again, no matter
how much she despised herself for it.

She had walked half the length of the paddock and
not seen anyone, when she caught sight of someone
coming from the stables mounted on the big grey stallion that Alex usually rode. The animal was unmistakable and she automatically assumed it would be Alex
who rode it, so that her immediate reaction was one of
pleasure.

Then she realised the truth and caught her breath
at the sight of Colin astride the broad back, his bony
young hands already having trouble controlling the big
brute, and his eyes noting her arrival with a gleam of
defiance. He came on, battling every inch of the way
with the stallion's determination to get the bit between
his teeth and go his own way, high-stepping, moving
sideways, and dangerous unless checked.

'Colin!' She met with him at the corner of the house,

but took care not to stand too close, frowning as sternly as she knew how. 'You're not up there with your father's permission, I'm quite sure,' she told him. 'Haven't you been——'

'I'm quite capable of handling him,' Colin interrupted defiantly. His cheeks were flushed and there was a bright challenging gleam in his grey eyes that made them very reminiscent of his father's, despite their colour. 'I'm nearly sixteen, you know, Carla,' he reminded her. 'I get a bit fed up with being treated like a child. Grey isn't so hard to handle, it's just that Alex likes to keep him for himself.' That small, tight and rather bitter smile was very like his father too. 'It's a *man*'s horse, you ken.'

'That's right, it is!' She looked at the bright, bold eyes of the stallion, and knew that Alex was right. He was the only one who could handle it; he was the only one with the physical strength and the sheer will-power to dominate a creature like that. And she wondered if it was simply youthful pride and the Hepburn stubbornness that made Colin either unable or unwilling to see it. 'Please, Colin,' she pleaded. 'Don't take chances just to try and prove something.'

There was an obstinate look on Colin's mouth that she knew only too well. 'I'm not taking chances,' he denied. Looking down at her, he hung on grimly to the reins. 'Why don't you come too, if you want to keep an eye on me?'

'I will!' It was one way of making sure he was under somebody's eye, even if it was only her own inexperienced one, and if she took time to go and tell Alex, Colin would be long gone before he came. 'Just hang on while I get Jenna saddled and I'll be with you.'

He nodded, though reluctantly, she realised, for the stallion was likely to prove much more difficult if he was required to stand and wait. She turned quickly and covered the few yards to the stable at a run, relieved to find the man who looked after the stables standing with a saddle over one arm and looking at her with a dour, enquiring expression on his face.

'Saddle Jenna for me, will you, please,' she said. 'I'm going out with Colin.'

The man inclined his head, carrying on into the stable building while he spoke. 'Somebody should go with him,' he observed grimly. 'He'll like as not break his neck on yon beast, but he's gey stubborn, an' I couldna shift him from it. He'd have Grey an' none other, an' it's no for me ta lay doon the law ta him.'

'I'll go with him and do what I can,' Carla promised. 'Is Mr Hepburn around?'

He wasn't, of course, or Colin would not be out there astride the huge Grey and likely to come to grief unless he was stopped. 'He's awa' inta Gibbert,' the man told her.

With Caroline Millar no doubt, Carla guessed, and clenched her hands tightly as the man led the little half-Arab mare out into the yard for her. 'Well, let Mrs Hepburn know,' she told him. 'And saddle one of the others, will you? Just in case Mr Hepburn comes back while we're gone.'

'Aye, ma'am!'

There may have been sarcasm in the man's voice, but it was of little importance whether or not he resented her giving him instructions as long as he did as she said. The mare was anxious to be off now that she smelled the freedom of the open country, and she responded to Carla's encouraging click with her tongue unhesitatingly.

It took only a glance to tell her that Colin had not done as she said and waited for her, for there was no sign of him, but whether or not he had been the one who decided, she had no way of knowing. More than

likely the stallion had taken matters into his own hands
and decided not to wait, and that was what worried her
as she started along the path beside the house.

She had got only as far as the corner of the house
when the Land-Rover pulled up and Alex got out. He
was frowning across at her curiously and, after a brief
glance at her face, he came hurrying over, holding the
mare's bridle with one hand while he looked up at
Carla.

'It's Colin,' she explained without giving him time
to say anything. 'He's taken Grey out, and I'm going to
try and get him to come back, although I don't have
much hope, the mood he was in.'

Alex said something fierce and to the point, then
reached up and lifted her bodily from the saddle. 'I'll
get him!' he told her shortly, and the grim set of his
mouth boded ill for Colin. 'If he's so keen on getting
his neck broken, I'll do it for him and save Grey the
trouble!'

Then he jabbed his heels into Jenna's sides with
such force that she flinched and her eyes were wild
with panic at the unexpected harshness as they went
flying along the paddock fence, making for the open
carse, her black mane flying like a banner in the wind,
while Carla stood watching them for a moment.

She turned swiftly when someone touched her elbow,
and turned to find the man standing behind her with
another animal already saddled, just as she had asked
for. She nodded her thanks when he handed her the
rein and helped her to mount, then looked up at her
with a dark and speculative eye.

'Ye'll catch up easy on this beauty if you've the mind
ta let her have her way,' he promised. 'She's twice the
speed o' yon wee creature Mr Hepburn's on, and she's
mair stamina too.'

He slapped the mare hard on the rump and stood back while Carla hung on, trying not to let the sheer strength and speed of her mount overwhelm her. It was so long since she had ridden, apart from that one time with Alex, and only her concern for Colin made her almost forget concern for herself as they galloped out over the short, lush turf in Alex's wake.

Despite what the stableman had told her, it was quite some time before she caught him up, and when she did there was still no sign of Colin on the stallion. Alex was standing in the stirrups in an attempt to widen his field of view, and he spared her only a brief glance when she came up to join him, thankfully pulling her own animal to a halt.

'Did you see which direction he took?' Alex asked her, and Carla shook her head.

'I asked him to wait for me while I had Jenna saddled, but he must have decided not to and just— took off.'

'Or Grey did,' Alex observed grimly. 'Yon beauty has a mind of his own, and he needs a firm hand or he goes his own way.' He cast around on the seemingly empty landscape once more then sat down and shook his head in angry frustration. 'Where the hell's that daft young limmer got to?' he demanded.

Worry and anger gave a harshness to his voice, and behind the dark gleaming fury in his eyes was a raw look of anxiety that tugged at her heart. It was just as if Colin and the big grey had vanished off the face of the earth, and she just did not see how it could have happened in the time.

As far as the blue hills in the distance, and the house with its neat gardens and white fencing; the wire fencing that kept the cattle from straying on to the road to the silver-grey serpent of river, there was no sign of them. She sank back on to the saddle, just as Alex had

done, then suddenly raised herself again and stared in
the direction of the fence that bordered the road, her
eyes narrowed and straining against the sunlight and
the distance.

'What's that over there?' Alex frowned, but followed
the direction of her pointing finger. 'I'm sure I can see
something——'

'Let's take a look!'

He jabbed the little mare into action again and she
leapt forward, followed closely by the one Carla rode.
Alex's voice reached her as she rode low, hanging on
for dear life as they raced towards the road, and she did
not trouble to answer the fiercely virulent vows of what
he would do to his son when he caught up with him.
For one thing she did not believe them.

The fence that controlled the cattle and kept them
from straying was made of strong, specially reinforced
wires strung between concrete posts, and beyond it was
a fairly wide grass verge before the road. Whatever it
was she had seen from that distant point, it had looked
like something grey, on the far side of the fencing, and
the nearer they got the more obvious it became what
had happened.

What had possessed Colin and the stallion to try and
jump it, heaven knew, but the attempt had failed and
the huge animal had come to grief. He lay on his side,
still winded and heaving in panic, but making no effort
to stand on his feet, so completely at odds with his
normal wild arrogance that it was unexpectedly touching. Colin lay nearly a couple of yards away, and
seemed to have come through the experience with less
damage.

He was conscious, but pale and still dazed, and he
looked up into his father's stern and anxious face with
tears in his eyes, no longer a boy trying to be a man, but
a boy pure and simple, with tearful eyes, bruised cheeks

and a trembling lip. 'Grey,' he said. 'He's hurt badly, Alex. I'm sorry.'

'We'll see just how sorry you will be,' his father promised him grimly, relief making him brutally angry. 'I'll teach you a lesson you won't forget, you disobedient young devil! Where are you hurt?'

Colin sat himself up, and from the way he moved it was clear he had suffered no serious injury. But he was pale and shaken and feeling very sorry for himself; although more sorry about Grey, Carla suspected. 'I was thrown clear and landed on this grass pile,' he explained to his father. 'But Grey caught the post with his leg and went down real heavy with his legs under him.' His face crumpled for a moment and he leaned his head against his father's shoulder. 'Och, I wish I'd broken *my* legs instead! I do, I wish it'd been me, not Grey!'

One large hand held him close for a moment, soothing and gentle, and Carla saw the look of love on Alex's hard, strong features when his face rested on the boy's dishevelled hair. 'Aye, I dare say,' he said, then caught Carla's eye when he eased Colin away and held him at arm's length. 'Carla, ride back to the Carse and ring Doctor Ellison and Tom McGaw, will you?'

'The vet?' She turned to obey even while she spoke, and when she looked back in the second before she put her heels to the willing mare, she saw Alex getting to his feet and going down on his knees beside the fallen stallion.

'Aye, the vet,' he said harshly. 'Hurry, girl!'

Without waiting any further bidding, Carla did as he said, urging the mare on, but with tears streaming down her face as she went, that she was trying to find a reason for. Colin was not too badly hurt, but the stallion was broken and helpless; no longer an animal worthy of the man who so often rode him. And she thought it was for Alex that she cried.

Tom was not pleased about her going back to the Carse after explaining her intention, but Carla had insisted that she wanted to be with Annie, even though the stalwart old lady showed no sign of wilting before the unexpected drama. She declared herself not too worried about her great-grandson, saying that he was a Hepburn and therefore made of tougher stuff than the average teenager. A wee toss from a horse, even a brute like Grey, was not going to do him much harm, she was confident of it.

And it seemed she was right, for the report from the hospital was that although they proposed keeping Colin in overnight for observation, there was actually little damage done. Alex had naturally gone with him, and he had telephoned the news as soon as he got it, but Carla could see that the old lady expected ructions the minute he came home.

In the meantime Carla sat with the old lady and tried to converse as normally as possible while all the time listening for Alex to come home. Sitting on a tapestry stool beside old Annie's chair, she found it hard to think about anything but that last sight she had had of Alex, on his knees between his son and his favourite mount. He had been angry and hurt, and she had felt an almost irresistible desire to comfort him even while he was ordering her to go for assistance.

It had not occurred to her until now to wonder where Caroline Millar might be. She had not been with Alex in the Land-Rover, and so far she had not put in an appearance in the sitting-room, so that Carla felt justified in asking after her. 'Where's Miss Millar this morning? Has she gone back?'

Annie eyed her rather curiously, she thought. 'Gone

back? No, hein, she's not been over yet today, though I don't doubt she'll be here sooner or later, she hasna missed a day yet.'

Carla eyed her for a moment, uncertain what to believe, but finally grasped the truth. 'You mean—you mean she isn't staying here?' she said.

'*Staying* here?' The shrewd old eyes regarded her narrowly. 'Why would she be doing that, when she has only to come from Mullen House?'

A big house on the way to Gibbert, Carla recalled dazedly. Huge and opulent, surrounded by trees and nothing like a working estate, such as Hepburn's Carse was. She could well imagine Caroline Millar living there, but it took her a moment or two to grasp the fact that the blonde woman was not staying under the same roof as Alex after all, and her own sense of relief stunned her.

'Archie Millar left here more than thirty years ago,' Annie went on. 'To make his fortune, so he said, and it seems like he succeeded, for he did not get Mullen House free wi' a packet of tea!' Carla's smile was purely instinctive, but it encouraged Annie to go on. 'He came back a year since with money to spare and a daughter who was looking for a husband, and decided she had found him the minute she clapped her een on Alex.' She looked round at Carla curiously. 'Whatever made you think she was staying here, girl?'

'I don't know.' Carla shrugged uneasily, then opened up under the old lady's sharp eye. 'I suppose because I thought there was something between her and Alex. And I was right about that at least.'

'Mebbe,' Annie allowed grudgingly. 'Unless some other lassie comes along and whisks him away from under her nose, which wouldna surprise me.' She chuckled, but there was more malice than amusement in the sound, Carla thought. 'Yon woman's not slow

to spot a guid man and if she's not to pin him down
somebody will have to move real sharp. She's a gift for
dangling the right bait too, and she's talking of putting money into the horse-breeding side of the business.'

It was disconcerting to have to do so much rethink-
ing on the character of Alex Hepburn lately, and Carla
wondered how many more surprises there were in store
for her. Her whole conception of him had had to
undergo a change in the past few days, so that she wondered if she had ever known the real man at all. This
latest revelation of Annie's was the most difficult of all
to accept, however, and she shook her head.

'You surely can't seriously mean he'd marry Miss
Millar just because she'll bring money to the estate,'
she said. 'He wouldn't, Annie—would he?'

A thin gentle hand stroked her hair, and Carla
looked up into her face anxiously. 'Och, he'd willingly
marry where his heart leads him, if he's given the
chance, I dare say,' Annie told her. 'He's an impulsive
man, hein, and sometimes hard to understand, but I
doubt not he'll go his own way as he did the first time.'
She patted Carla's cheek and smiled. 'He needs a wife
and more bairns, that is all I know, and no doubt in
his own guid time he'll do something about it. But
what about your situation, Carla, eh? Is yon man still
sharing your house?'

'Tom's still there,' Carla said, 'though I don't know
for how much longer now that the hotel plans have
fallen through.'

'And will you be going back with him? Marrying
him, mebbe?'

For some reason she did not altogether understand,
Tom still seemed like a safe refuge when she needed to
hide from Annie's probing. So instead of telling her
that she had made it quite clear to Tom that she wasn't

going to marry him, she prevaricated further; shaking her head and smiling ruefully. 'I haven't decided yet, Annie.'

'But now that you'll not be using the house for an hotel——'

'I'm not parting with it, Annie!' She spoke up quickly, knowing very well what Annie wanted to hear and refusing to say anything that the old lady could later construe as a promise.

'Ah, well,' Annie said, without the rebuke Carla had steeled herself for, 'there's no special rush, I daresay. Alex is a patient man.'

'Annie, I didn't say——'

'No, no,' Annie agreed soothingly, 'but you'd not let anyone else have it when you know your granddaddy wanted it to go to Alex, would you?'

Smiling resignedly, Carla looked up at her. 'You just never give up, do you?' she said. 'Making sure that Alex gets everything he wants, just as he always has. No wonder he's the—the arrogant man he is; he's never had reason to doubt his own ability to get what he wants, one way or another! All right——' She laughed a little unsteadily. 'I promise that if anyone has it, it will be Alex. Does that satisfy you? Now please can we talk about something else?'

'Och aye,' Annie agreed blithely. 'I've your promise and that's guid enough. But you'll not mind, will you,' she added, 'if I tell him that? A wee bit of reassurance, you know.'

Anxious only to have the subject finished with, Carla shook her head. 'No, I don't mind; you tell him if you want to.'

'I will then,' said Annie, settling back in her chair and closing her eyes for a second or two. 'He'll be gey glad to hear it.'

Both she and Carla sat up quickly and listened when

a vehicle stopped outside, and a few moments later heavy footsteps came across the hall. A heavy, impatient and unmistakable tread that brought a sudden swift urgency to Carla's heartbeat. Seconds later the door of the sitting-room opened and Alex came in, staring in momentary surprise when he saw Carla there.

He was still angry, but it was a dark smouldering anger that burned deep inside him, and he ran a hand through his hair as he sat down in an armchair and crossed his long legs at the ankle, stretching them out in front of him. In response to his grandmother's anxious gaze, he shook his head and sat himself upright, clasping his hands together.

'Colin's going to be perfectly all right,' he told her. 'He could have come home with me, but it was better if he stayed under observation for the one night.' Annie nodded agreement, and there was a taut kind of silence in the big room for several minutes. 'Damn it, I'm going to have to take him in hand!' Alex exploded suddenly, and with a smoulderingly defiant glare at the old lady. 'Whatever you say for him, Grandmother, he's been getting more and more stubborn and difficult every day of the last twelve months, and if he won't respond to the gentle touch, then he'll have to learn the hard way!'

'Like one of your horses?' Carla surprised herself by speaking up before Annie could reply, and from the corner of her eye she noted the old lady's curiously satisfied nod.

Alex too was surprised by her intervention, but he seemed not to resent it any more than his grandmother did, though he was angry still. 'The basic principle's the same, if you insist,' he told her harshly. 'Except that I've never had as much trouble teaching respect and good manners to one of my horses as I have trying to teach my son! I've never found it necessary to use a heavy hand, but Colin, it seems, is less amenable to persuasion!'

'Oh, Alex, don't be so hard on him!' Carla looked across at the darkly-tanned face with its gleaming eyes and wondered where she found the nerve from to argue with him in this mood. 'Colin's young; he's growing up and he needs guidance and understanding, not—not beating!'

'*Guidance?*' The brown eyes scorned her opinion, but she sensed the hurt behind his anger too, and particularly after his next words. 'How do I guide a boy who even resents my being here? He never takes a bit of notice of anything I say to him, but acts as if I've no right to even be here, let alone try to teach him anything!'

'He'll—change.'

She did not know it for certain, and even if it was true, Alex was in no mood at the moment to accept it. 'You'd think he would accept the fact that Grey is too strong for him to handle, and God knows I've told him over and over that he's not to ride him without I'm there to oversee, but he just had to prove that he's as good as I am!'

'I didn't know you let him ride Grey when you were with him,' Carla said, and chalked up another unexpected discovery about this intriguing man. 'He did say that—well, that you'd forbidden him to take Grey, and he was determined to prove he could handle him.'

'Damned little idiot! He's as stubborn as a mule and twice as much trouble, and for two pins I'd take it out of his hide the minute he comes home tomorrow!'

'Oh no, Alex!'

He looked at her steadily and something in the depth of his eyes sent shivering little flutters of sensation all along her spine. 'Oh, you find me a very hard

man, don't you, Carla?' he said in a flat cold voice, and
she hastily lowered her eyes.

'I didn't say that—I just don't think you understand
Colin very well, that's all. Even if he is your son.'

'You mean that business about becoming a vet, I suppose?' She nodded without speaking, then looked up
quickly when he got to his feet in a swift jerky movement, and stood looking down at her. 'Well, if that's
what he wants, he'd better have a stronger stomach
than I have! I've just had to stand by while Tom
McGaw put a bullet into my favourite horse, and I felt
physically sick!'

He turned abruptly and walked out of the room
with old Annie's eyes following him, looking as close to
tears as Carla had ever seen her. 'Puir Alex,' she said
softly, and Carla turned and looked at her, making no
attempt to conceal her own tears.

'I didn't think about Grey being put down,' she
whispered. 'Oh, Annie, how could I have forgotten
how he loved that great brute? Will he ever forgive
me?'

A long bony hand stroked her hair gently. 'Aye, of
course he will, hein,' Annie told her. 'But for the
moment leave him with his grief, for he'd not want you
to see him now.'

Nor would he, Carla realised, for he was not a man
to let on how much he could grieve. Maybe he would
not want her to sympathise after her attack on his deal-
ings with his son, but she would try. She *had* to try.

CHAPTER SIX

IT was a couple of days later, when Carla was clearing away after lunch, that she spotted someone coming slowly along the garden path, and she assumed, when she noticed the movement from the corner of her eye, that it was Tom. He was outside somewhere, ostensibly doing something to the car, but he invariably disappeared whenever there was any kind of domestic work to be done, so that she doubted the validity of the excuse.

She frowned in confusion when she realised it was strangers making their leisurely way along the overgrown path, and thanked heaven that Tom wasn't too far away, when she saw the type of people they were. It was a man and a woman, and something about them made Carla immediately suspicious.

The man was small and thin and she noticed how he glanced to right and left of him as he came slouching through the overgrown garden, as if he feared being followed. The woman was plumper, but no more prepossessing, and both were very evidently strangers to soap and water. They spotted her at the kitchen window a while before they reached the door, and stared at her boldly for a second or two before shifting their gaze to the ground at their feet.

If there had been any way of ignoring them after that, Carla would have done so, but there was nothing she could do now but have the door already open by the time they got there and try to look more confident than she felt. It was only when they were on the doorstep and the woman raised her eyes for just a second to

look at her directly that Carla began to realise who
they could be, and her heart clamoured wildly in panic.

Set in a round face between red, lashless rims, the
woman's eyes were a light, cool grey, and uncannily like
Colin's. Almost without doubt the pair were his grandparents, and had decided to try their luck at Hepburn's
Quay without waiting to see if their promised cottage
suited them better. Colin must have said something to
them, and she could only hope that he had not been too
encouraging.

'You'll be Miss Francis, will you?' the man enquired
in the sibilant, ingratiating tone of his kind. 'Oor
name's McKinnon; Colin Hepburn is oor grandson,
ye ken.'

'Oh yes—yes, of course. How are you?'

Carla did not smile. To smile, she felt would be to
encourage them, and she dared not do that. But the
man was eyeing her slyly from below sparse sandy
lashes. 'The laddie said ye'd a fine house here,' he told
her with a faint leer, 'an' that ye were a guid-hearted
kind o' woman.'

Carla doubted if Colin had been so profuse, but she
wished he had not mentioned her at all to these people,
for she could not see them being easy to discourage. 'I
was very glad to hear about your cottage,' she ventured,
hoping to put them right on that matter first. 'It must
be a weight off your minds to have somewhere more to
your liking.'

It was possible that they thought her in ignorance of
that fact, and from the man's frown it looked as if she
was right. 'Ah, weel now,' he said, shaking his head.
'It's an awfu' long way from here, ye ken, an' the carse
has always been oor place.' The small sly eyes watched
her for some kind of reaction, and narrowed slightly
when there was none. 'Colin said ye'd be willing for us
ta come an' live here,' he went on and, seeing that her

husband was making no headway, the woman decided to take a hand.

'Will ye no ask us in?' she said, and her grey eyes had a curious chilling quality that Colin's never had.

Carla glanced along to the corner of the house, almost praying for Tom to put in an appearance, but there was no sign of him. He was keeping himself well hidden while she washed up the lunch things. Seeing nothing else for it, she stepped back and allowed them into the big warm kitchen, turning to follow them in.

'Ye'll have a deal o' room here, eh?' Blane McKinnon guessed, and leered at her knowingly. 'An' just you an' ye're mon, I hear tell?' He cocked his bird-like head to one side and eyed her narrowly. 'The mon's not here?' he asked, quite confident he knew the answer.

'Yes, he is, in fact,' Carla assured him hastily. 'He's just outside, in the byre where we keep the car.'

'Is that right?' From the way he glared at his wife it was pretty clear who had decided that Carla was alone. 'Weel now, Miss Francis, ye telt the laddie that ye'd find us room, me an' ma woman. An' we're here ta tell ya that we like the idea o' livin' in a hoose like this yin.'

'Oh, but you——' Carla stared at them, swallowing her moment of panic hastily. 'You've been found another cottage, Colin told me. You have no need to come here now; I made that offer only to try and help out when I thought you were being put into a town house. The cottage——'

'A place found by yon Hepburn!' the man declared spitefully, and left his feelings for his son-in-law in no doubt at all. He glared at her with small narrowed eyes. 'He's wantin' to have us far away from his son, that's *his* guid heart for ye! An, the laddie oor ain grandson, mind!'

Carla understood perfectly, and her sympathies lay entirely with Alex. Grandparents or not, the less Colin

saw of these people the better. 'I'm sorry.' She tried to
sound firm and unyielding. 'But you have somewhere
to go and I can't have you here after all—things have
changed.'

'Aye,' the man said, twisting his slack mouth into an
ugly leer, 'yon Hepburn aye had a way o' persuadin'
lassies ta do what he wanted. We ken that weel
enough!'

Carla blushed furiously, unable to forget the heart-
stopping effect of Alex's kiss out there by the river. But
she thrust it determinedly to the back of her mind and
looked at him with all the scorn she could muster. 'I
make up my own mind about things that concern my
property, Mr McKinnon,' she told him firmly. 'I can't
take you here, and you have a cottage to go to instead
of a town house, so just thank heaven that you did better out of it than you expected.'

'Be grateful, is it?' McKinnon demanded, and took
a step towards her, his eyes narrowed maliciously.

Heaven knew what he intended to do, but Carla saw
his face change suddenly and a moment after that Tom
came in through the door, stopping short when he saw
the visitors and frowning curiously. The smaller man
subsided for a moment while he weighed up the situation, but Carla had never welcomed anyone so warmly
in her life as she did Tom at that moment.

'Oh, Tom, I'm glad you're here!' She tried hard to
control not only her voice but her trembling legs as
she turned and smiled at him thankfully. 'This is Mr
and Mrs McKinnon, Colin's grandparents. Mr Laxey.'

In the circumstances a formal introduction seemed
almost ludicrous, and for just a second Carla was
threatened with rising hysteria on top of everything
else. Quick to size up any situation, Tom knew exactly
what was going on and he moved up close beside her,
one hand holding hers and his eyes fixed on the couple
who faced her. Rather surprisingly it was the woman

who spoke up first, her chilling grey eyes on Tom.

'This'll be ye're mon?' she enquired.

'I'm Miss Francis's guest and business partner,' Tom informed her with gratifying aplomb, and gave Carla's courage the boost it badly needed. 'Is there any special reason for this visit, Mrs McKinnon?'

It obviously wasn't the response that was expected, but the woman was not put out for very long. 'A promise is why we're here!' she shrilled at him after a second's hesitation. 'Yon woman made a promise ta Colin, oor grandson, that she'd gie us room in her hoose, an' we're here ta take her up on it!'

'But hasn't Miss Francis explained?' Tom asked quietly. 'She isn't in a position to take you in; circumstances have changed, and it's no longer possible. I'm sorry.'

'And are you the master here?' Mrs McKinnon demanded aggressively.

Tom's hand tightened its hold on Carla and betrayed more than anything the seething anger he kept so well under control. 'As far as you're concerned, I am,' he said coolly. 'And I'd be obliged if you'd leave now that the situation has been made clear to you.'

'No sae fast, ma mannie!' Tom flushed at the derisive smirk on the man's dusky features. 'The lassie here is near kin, wi' her bein' a Hepburn like oor Isabella, an' she made a promise ta Colin, she cannae deny it!'

No one heard a sound outside, but the group in the kitchen became oddly still suddenly when a long dark shadow loomed across the tiled floor from the doorway, and Blane McKinnon's small shifty eyes darted uneasily to the source of it. Not only McKinnon, but Tom and Carla too, and Mrs McKinnon's chilling grey eyes turned to where Alex stood in the doorway with the afternoon sun behind him.

Carla's instinctive sense of relief at his appearance

was tempered with caution when she noticed the way
he looked. He must have ridden over from Hepburn's
Carse, for they would surely have heard the Land-
Rover, and he had an air of menace about him as well
as a dark brooding anger that gleamed in his eyes.
Carla felt herself trembling, but it was to the McKinnons he addressed himself first, not to her.

'Save your breath and get out of here, McKinnon,' he
told the man with almost brutal contempt. 'You're
wasting your time; there's no chance of you coming
here, nor ever was!'

Carla had to hand it to the man, he was prepared to
try just once more, even in the face of such fierce op-
position. 'It was a promise that——' he began, but fell
silent when Alex laughed harshly.

'Och, don't heed promises from *this* young lady,' he
told him. 'You'll find they're too easily broken!'

Carla would have objected, and indeed she moved
away from Tom's protective arm and stepped towards
Alex, but before she could speak he unfolded a paper
he had in his hand and thrust it under Blane McKinnon's nose. While the little man peered at it helplessly,
making it clear that he could not read what was there,
Alex turned his eyes on Carla—a gaze so deep and dark
and furiously angry that she shivered.

'That will tell you just how reliable Miss Francis's
promises are!' he declared forcefully.

But if McKinnon was unable to read the paper,
Carla could, and she felt Tom's hand reach out for
her as she leaned forward. Printed in bold black print
on blue paper, the words swam before her eyes, but she
got the gist of them easily enough, and stared in blank
disbelief. She knew now why Tom had been so relieved
when she told him she was not having the McKinnons
there after all, and what he meant by giving her a
slight shove in the right direction.

'The place has been put up for auction, to be sold in

a month's time,' Alex explained for his father-in-law's benefit. 'You've been fooled, just as I have, McKinnon, fooled by promises! What do you do about a woman who makes promises she has no intention of keeping, eh? Tell me that! How do you trust her?'

Too stunned to say anything, Carla simply stared, and she dared not look at Tom. The McKinnons were out of their depth completely, but it was clear that they held their son-in-law in awe, even though they hated him; or possibly envied rather than hated. Carla felt her legs becoming so unsteady they threatened to let her down and she wished she still had Tom to cling to, especially when those darkly menacing eyes turned on her again.

'I never gave you credit for being as—devious as you obviously are,' he told her in a flat, cold voice. 'I thought I knew you!'

The words seemed to strike directly at Carla's heart and she could find nothing to say, that was the worst part, not even in her own defence. Alex screwed up the poster into a tight ball and flung it down on the floor, then turned and went striding out of the door and into the sunshine once more. It was a second or two before Carla realised she was crying, and she could do nothing about it.

Carla was angry and she made no attempt to conceal it. The moment she and Tom were alone she had turned on him with the fury of a wildcat, and demanded to know by what right he made arrangements for the sale of her property without her knowledge. Perhaps Tom realised that it was the memory of Alex's lean, angry figure striding out of the kitchen in disgust at what he saw as her double-dealing that made her so angry, or maybe he didn't, but he said little to justify himself initially.

'I suppose this was what you meant by a gentle

nudge in the right direction?' she said, standing across the kitchen table from him, and Tom shrugged.

'I did,' he admitted quietly. 'I didn't expect you to take it like this, Carla.'

'Oh, you——' Hands pressed to either side of her face, she raised her eyes to heaven in appeal. 'How did you *expect* me to take it? You know I don't want to part with the house, so you surely didn't expect it would please me to find out you'd gone ahead and done it behind my back, did you?'

He was sitting on one of the kitchen chairs, facing her and looking suitably contrite, and yet something lurked at the back of his eyes that suggested he was not quite as sorry as he professed to be. 'I'm sorry you got so upset about it, darling, but I was trying to help you to make up your mind. You didn't seem to know what you wanted, and you can't stay on here alone after I've gone back to London, so——'

'I *can* stay on,' Carla argued. 'Although it's unlikely I'll be very popular with my relatives now that you've given them the impression I intend to break my word. I solemnly promised Annie that if anyone else got Hepburn's Quay, it would be Alex, and calling off the auction isn't going to mean anything to her except that I've been caught out in an underhand attempt to break my promise.'

Tom had not known about that, in all fairness, but to Carla's mind that was no excuse for what he had done, and she was not in a particularly magnanimous mood at the moment. 'I seem to have got a little out of line,' Tom conceded, 'and I'm sorry about it.' For a moment he eyed her flushed face, then raised a questioning brow. 'But if you don't want it put into the auction, what *do* you plan to do with it?'

It took her a moment or two to come to a decision,

then she shook her head slowly. 'I'll offer it to Alex, if he still wants it.'

His eyes gleamed suddenly and he leaned towards her eagerly. 'Does that mean you'll be coming back to town with me after all?'

'It means,' Carla told him a little wearily, 'that it's the only way I can think of to make Alex realise I wasn't breaking my word about letting him have the house.'

Tom regarded her steadily and his feelings were quite plain. 'Does that matter so much?' he asked quietly, and instead of meeting his eyes, Carla shrugged uneasily.

'What else can I do?'

Reaching across, Tom took her hands and pressed them tightly in his. 'Marry me and forget all about this place,' he urged. 'You'll be much better off, darling.'

'No, Tom!' She sounded quite adamant, and she ignored the way he looked when she snatched her hands free and walked across to the door. Leaning against the door frame, she looked along the length of the overgrown garden to the little granite quay. 'I want to stay here at least for a while. If I do anything in too much of a hurry I might regret it—I've done things on impulse too often and lived to regret it.'

She heard the chair he was sitting on scrape back on the tiled floor, and seconds later the warmth of his body was immediately behind her, a hand sliding around her waist. 'Does that include coming up here with me?' he asked and, when she did not reply, sighed deeply. 'I suppose you realise that if you *do* let cousin Alex have it after all, you won't find him a very charitable land-lord after the way you've given him the run-around? What happens then?'

Carla half-turned her head and looked at him, wondering if she knew the answer to that herself. Then she smiled ruefully and shook her head, admitting defeat. 'I haven't worked that one out yet,' she confessed. 'But I don't think Alex would hold a grudge, and he'd let me stay here for a little while at least.'

And she felt sure he would, although the mood Alex had been in when he left, he would probably turn down any suggestion that came from her. In any event she meant to see him and explain, however unwilling he was to listen. As Tom had intimated, it was important to her to make Alex see her side of it.

She simply told Tom the following morning that she was going visiting; he would know where she was going and why. She had taken trouble with her appearance quite deliberately, and the white lawn blouse she wore with a dark green cotton skirt was dainty and feminine, and had a flatteringly low neckline that hinted lovingly at the soft curves below the deep vee. And she left her hair loose too so that it framed her face in the most flattering way possible. If she was going to make her peace with Alex she wanted to appear as appealing as she could, although it was only when she noted the way Tom looked at her that she realised how well she had succeeded.

It had rained the night before, and as she walked along the path beside the loch the ground smelled gloriously rich and spicy, her footsteps adding to the scent each time she trod and bruised the damp heather and turf underfoot. Little clumps of earth clung to the soles of her shoes and made her wish she had put something more substantial on her feet, but she paid little heed, anticipating her next meeting with Alex.

There was a horse box parked at the far end of the paddock, she saw, and a man was securing the end door while he talked to Alex. The horses were a profitable sideline, Annie had told her, and she could believe it, for they were beautiful creatures and well bred. The magnificent and late-lamented Grey had sired them all, and for the first time Carla understood that Alex had lost not only a favourite mount but a valuable part of his business as well when the big stallion was killed.

The horse box was being driven off when she reached the gate, but Alex barely looked up at her approach, concentrating instead on fastening the paddock gate securely. Using the departing horse box as an opening gambit, she watched after it, instead of looking at him. This was going to be a difficult conversation and she had yet to establish whether or not he would even deign to talk to her. He could no longer pretend to be fixing the big metal catch when she came up beside him, and he turned his head briefly to look at her.

'Hello, Alex. You've made a sale?'

'One of the mares.'

He answered her in a cool deep voice that showed no sign of anger or resentment. It was simply offhand and casual, almost too uncaring, and he did not return her greeting, she noticed. He was going to make it difficult for her, but she had been prepared for that, and she simply went ahead determinedly. She had her share of Hepburn stubbornness too.

'Did you get a good price for her?' she asked, leaning her arms on the fence.

'Good enough.' He made no more pretence of being occupied, but turned a long steady look on her. 'Did you come to see Grandmother? If so you'll find her at the house.'

He would have gone stalking off after that, but she couldn't let him go before she had even mentioned the reason she came, and she called after him before he had gone more than a couple of steps. 'I came to see you, Alex, not Annie!' He stopped, then turned and fixed her once more with that steady and very discouraging gaze. 'Oh, don't look at me as if I was something dredged up from the loch, Alex!' Her voice shook with mingled anxiety and impatience. 'I want to talk to you, to explain. I want to put things right about the house, and the least you can do is listen to me!'

He did not come back, but stood where he was with one hand in a pocket, and waited. 'I'm listening,' he said.

It was even more difficult now that she had his full attention, and that steady, heavy-lidded scrutiny did not make matters any easier. She thrust both hands into the front pockets of her skirt and watched her own foot poking a stone around on the ground instead of looking at him. 'It's about that matter of the auction,' she began, and glanced up briefly to see if that made any impression.

'Naturally!'

She squirmed in frustration at his deliberate sarcasm, and the warning glint was in her green eyes, if only he heeded it. 'Tom organised it without my knowledge or my permission—will you believe that?'

The slight flutter of half-closed lids was the only indication that she might have surprised him, but Carla welcomed any sign that he did not simply dismiss her claim to innocence out of hand. 'Mebbe he thought he had the right to in the circumstances,' he suggested, and Carla frowned at him.

'Well, he hadn't!'

There was a look in his eyes that brought a swift flush of colour to her cheeks. 'He's in love with you,' he said, without allowing a shadow of doubt about it. 'But you know that well enough, of course.'

He was leading the conversation off at a tangent and she wanted to stay with the subject of her errand. 'Yes, I know,' she admitted. 'But that doesn't excuse him trying to sell the Quay without my knowledge. I'd promised Annie that you should have it if anyone did.'

'She told me.'

'Then you should have known I wasn't responsible for arranging to sell it by auction,' she reproached him. 'I wouldn't break my word to *you*.'

The slight stress on that last word had been quite unintentional, but she felt a curious sense of excitement stirring in her when she glanced up. First at the tall, lean length of him and then, more slowly, at his face. He was watching her with a steady dark gaze, and she held his eyes for a moment with a boldness she would never have believed herself capable of, then the tip of her tongue darted swiftly across her lips before she lowered her lashes.

'Don't you know me better than that, Alex?'

A couple of short steps was all it needed to bring him close to where she stood with her back to the paddock fence, and with her eyes downcast she saw only the toes of his booted feet at first. They were set firmly on the muddy ground in front of her, slightly apart and unshifting even when she made a slight move, as if to get past him. The lean warmth of him was heart-stoppingly close and he slid a hand beneath the hair at her nape, long fingers commandingly gentle when they turned her towards him and tilted her chin.

'I once knew a young and very impressionable girl— a schoolgirl,' he said in his deep and softly accented voice, and the ball of his thumb slid back and forth with hypnotic regularity over her skin. 'What I am faced with now is a woman who looks at me as if——' He shook his head slowly. 'Was it so important to come here and convince me, Carla?'

'I thought it was.'

Her voice was low and breathlessly unsteady and by instinct she turned her face to the warmth of his hand, thick brown lashes brushing her cheeks. His long fingers curved, cupping her cheek and stroking lightly

over her soft skin. 'So you put on your prettiest blouse,
let your hair down like a wanton in the wind and came
to see me?' Something in his voice made her look up at
him again, her lips parted in vague surprise. Alex bent
his head and kissed her, his mouth lingering, warming
her lips with his breath. 'Does he know you're here?'
he asked. 'That man who shares your house?'

'Alex?'

She leaned back from him, frowning slightly and disturbed by his manner; by an inexplicable harshness in
his voice. Then his hard fingers tightened on her neck,
holding her firm while he looked down into her eyes, his
own dark and gleaming.

'I believe you really didn't know your boy-friend had
sneaked behind your back and tried to sell the Quay,'
he said, 'so you've achieved that much at least by coming to see me. But by God, I feel sorry for the poor
devil!'

Carla caught her breath and looked up at him with
wide, unbelieving eyes. 'I don't understand you, Alex.'

'D'you not?' The hand at the nape of her neck slid
away, leaving only the impression of its warmth on
her skin, and his heavy-lidded eyes were dark and unfathomable. He stepped back, thrusting both hands
into his pockets. 'I'd not like to think *my* girl was giving another man the kind of signals you're sending me,'
he told her harshly. 'Grandmother said you were havering about whether to marry him or no, but by God, he
must be half out of his mind by now, living under the
same roof with you and not knowing which way you're
going to turn!'

'Alex——'

'I tell you,' Alex went on inexorably, 'you'd not have
got away with dangling the bait in front of *me* for this
long, my girl! I'd have put you firmly in your place
long since!'

'Alex, stop it!' He had, Carla realised, got hold of entirely the wrong idea, but she curled up under the scathing look he gave her before he turned away. 'You —you don't understand. You can have Hepburn's Quay—it's yours if you still want it. That's what I came to tell you!'

He turned again and she met the brown eyes full on, her pulse thudding hard at her temple. A fierce passion burned in him and gave his eyes the hard, gleaming brightness of agates. 'Why?' he asked quietly, after a moment or two. 'What made you change your mind? Why now, suddenly, Carla?'

She was trembling like a leaf and her voice was little more than a breathless whisper when she told him. 'It's a—a kind of act of good faith,' she ventured. 'To convince you that I had nothing to do with the auction idea.'

Alex said nothing for a moment, then he shook his head slowly. 'I'd like to be a whole lot more sure that you mean it before I start thanking you,' he told her, and Carla bit her lip in frustration at such a disappointing response.

'I mean it,' she assured him. 'I—I'd just like to live there for a little while longer, that's all. After that——'

She shrugged, leaving him to draw his own conclusions, but Alex was still disappointingly unresponsive. 'I'll take it, for the full market price,' he said eventually, and far less graciously than Carla felt entitled to expect. 'But don't think you can have second thoughts about it in the morning, because you won't find *me* easy to play games with, Carla. I'm no lovesick loon to be kept on a knife edge while you haver about making up your mind.'

'Alex, you have no right——'

'No,' Alex interrupted shortly, 'I haven't!'

He turned his back to her once more, dismissing her

with a brief wave of his hand and a murmured word or
two, then went striding off back towards the house. But
something about the expression in his eyes in the
moment before he turned from her stirred unbidden
excitements in her, because she recognised something
more than merely anger or contempt.

She was shaking like a leaf when she eventually
turned to go, and it was a second or two before she
realised what lay ahead, in the near distance at Hepburn's Quay. Stopping short, she stared in horror at
billowing spumes of black smoke that seemed to come
from the old byre where Tom kept the car. And even
while she watched great vivid tongues of flame darted
skyward through the blackness, rising higher every
second. Her cry was instinctive and shrill with urgency.

'Alex!'

Whatever he had felt on parting from her, Alex was
beside her almost at once, and he acted as she would
expect him to; quickly and concisely. 'Go to the house
and call the fire brigade,' he told her, and as he gave the
order he turned her forcibly, for she seemed to have
become rooted to the spot, then dragged her along
with him as he ran back towards the house. 'Come on,
hurry, while I get the Land-Rover!'

Her legs moved obediently, even though they felt
too weak to support her, and she tried to explain the
reason for her fears as she ran, her voice thin and
breathless. 'It's coming from the byre,' she gasped, 'and
Tom's in there tinkering with the car——'

'Save your breath for the phone,' Alex ordered
shortly, and let go her arm to run off in the direction
of the garage. 'I'll go down and do what I can until the
brigade gets there!'

Just for a second they both stopped dead in their
tracks when the quiet was shattered violently by an
explosion, and Carla stared in horrible disbelief at the

red glow in the pale summer sky above old Annie's apple trees. Her heart seemed to have stopped beating, and her legs were incapable of movement, but once more Alex galvanised her into action, yelling at her in a flat harsh voice that made no allowances for shocking speculation.

'Move, girl, and make that call! Go on, damn you, have you taken root?'

Dazedly she turned and ran into the house, but even while she was dialling the number with trembling fingers, she wondered what she would have done without him. She dared not think about what might be happening to Tom, but she glanced up as a crisply efficient voice piped against her ear, and heard the Land-Rover go racing past. And suddenly her fears were for Alex.

When Carla saw how much damage had been done by the fire, she marvelled that anyone could have come out of the old byre alive, and yet Tom had. He was suffering from superficial burns and he was still in Gibbert hospital, but he had been incredibly lucky. Carla's visits to him were very much dependent upon Alex being available, for he had insisted that she did not take a taxi, but allowed him to drive her there. In the circumstances she did not like to ask, and so it was left for him to come over and offer to take her.

He had insisted that she at least sleep over at Hepburn's Carse too, and she had yielded on that readily enough, but she did no more than sleep there, and the rest of the time she carried on as usual. Until Tom came out of hospital, she was living in a kind of vacuum, waiting for something to happen and doing nothing at all about Hepburn's Quay or her own future for the moment.

So far she had not thought very much about what had actually caused the fire, for she had been too con-

cerned for the victim of it, but she realised that sooner
or later the question would have to be answered. In
fact the subject was raised rather sooner and in a much
different way from what she anticipated.

When she heard a car stop, three or four days after
the incident, she quite expected to see Alex, and called
out to him to come in almost before there was a knock
on the door. Instead of coming in, however, the caller
knocked again and she was frowning curiously when
she went to open the door. For a moment she stared
blankly at the man who stood there, vaguely murmur-
ing an automatic response to his greeting.

'Miss Francis?' She nodded, and he produced a card
from his inside pocket and showed it to her. 'I'd like
a word with you, if I may, Miss Francis.'

'Oh yes. Yes, of course.' She stepped back quickly to
allow him into the kitchen, but her heart was hammering anxiously as she followed him in, for she could not
imagine why a police officer should be calling on her.
There could surely be nothing suspicious about the fire,
and that was the only out-of-the-ordinary event to have
happened lately. 'How can I help you?' she asked.

The man walked across to the kitchen window and
looked out. It was not possible to see the charred re-
mains of the byre from there because of the overgrown
hedges and the corner of the house. In fact the byre
was not, strictly speaking, at the back of the house,
but to one side. Carla watched him uneasily while he
checked the view from the window and gave him only
a very uncertain smile when he turned back into the
room.

'You cannot see the byre from here,' he said, and she
shook her head, indicating a chair for him, for her own
legs felt strangely weak suddenly and she needed to sit
down.

'I shouldn't have seen it start anyway,' Carla told

him. 'I wasn't here, I was over at the Carse.'

'Ooh aye.' He glanced through a small notebook that he laid on the table-top. 'You were lucky the fire didn't reach the house.' He had the same quiet and softly accented voice that her grandfather had had, and the rest of the Hepburns, and she found it oddly comforting in the present circumstances. 'You'll be insured, of course, Miss Francis?'

Carla looked at him vaguely for a second, then shook her head. 'I honestly don't know,' she confessed. 'I suppose my grandfather must have taken out an insurance, but I haven't thought about it since I took over.' She watched him make a brief note in his book, then went on quickly and rather breathlessly. 'I don't quite understand why *you're* here,' she said. 'I mean, why on earth would the police be interested in a little fire like this?'

'It's normal practice in the case of any fire where the brigade is called out, miss. And there are one or two things I have to ask you.' He smiled at her briefly. 'Nothing to worry about, just a few questions that need answers, and since it's your property——' He looked up for a moment, still smiling. 'It *is* your property, is it not, Miss Francis?'

'Oh yes.' She moistened her lips with the tip of her tongue, not quite sure why she was so nervous, and hoping it was not giving the wrong impression to the softly spoken man who sat facing her. 'I inherited it from my grandfather, Mr Fergus Hepburn.'

He nodded. 'And what exactly has the old byre been used for, miss?'

Instead of answering him, Carla looked up quickly at the familiar sound of Alex's Land-Rover drawing up by the gate, and her heart was racing hopefully, thankful that he was there without being entirely sure why she needed him so much. Then, followed by the policeman's faintly speculative eye, she hurried across to welcome Alex with what was obviously unexpected warmth.

'Oh, Alex, I'm so glad you've come!' She clasped her two hands over his bare brown arm and looked up at him as they crossed the kitchen. 'I've got a policeman here asking me about the fire, and I can't imagine why.'

'Just routine, hein, that's all.' He patted her hand in a kindly, almost avuncular way, then eased away from her clasp, greeting the stranger amiably. 'Good morning, Sergeant Muir. This has fallen to your lot, then?'

Whether or not the policeman welcomed his arrival was hard to say, but they obviously knew one another fairly well, and the two of them exchanged pleasantries for a second or two before the sergeant returned to business. 'Well now, Miss Francis, shall we go on?' He consulted his notes again. 'Mr Thomas Laxey, the man who was injured, he lives here?' She nodded, but avoided Alex's eyes as she did so. 'And would the gentleman be a smoker at all?' Again she nodded. 'What exactly did you keep out there in the byre?'

Carla thought for a moment, then shrugged. 'The car, of course, and a few cardboard boxes we found in the attics; and some straw that must have been there from the time the byre was used for cattle.'

'That's all?' She nodded, but could not miss the significance of the question asked in the same soft, gentle voice. 'You're quite sure about that, Miss Francis?'

'Quite sure,' Carla insisted, then caught her lower lip between her teeth suddenly. 'As far as I know there was nothing else,' she said, qualifying her earlier insistence in the interests of strict accuracy. 'I mean, there might have been some old tools and things like that, I can't exactly remember. You see, I only went out there a couple of times, no more. Tom always looked at the car and drove it in and out, I had no call to go out there after the first time.'

'You don't remember anything stored in drums?' He noticed her puzzled frown and enlarged on his meaning. 'Like oil, perhaps, or paraffin?'

Carla shook her head. 'No, nothing like that, sergeant. I'm sure I'd have noticed if there had been. Tom—Mr Laxey will be able to tell you more than I can; he spent a lot of time out there tinkering with the car.'

'Ah!'

Alex sat a little apart from them, in the old-fashioned beechwood armchair by the fireplace, as if he held no more than a watching brief. But he caught the other man's eye suddenly and obviously read some significance into that brief exclamation. 'What's in the air, sergeant?' he asked. 'I know this is Miss Francis's concern, strictly speaking, but it's all family, as you appreciate.'

'Aye, aye,' the sergeant allowed gently, and he seemed much more ready to enlighten Alex than her. 'The fact is, the inspector has come up with some rather puzzling evidence, Mr Hepburn. There was an explosion, was there not?'

'Yes, there was,' Alex agreed readily. 'But when the fire reached the petrol tank of the car it *would* explode, surely?' He eyed the sergeant narrowly for a second, then came up with his own conclusion. 'Something more than that?'

Sergeant Muir nodded. 'Aye, sir, a deal more, you might say. The young lady says she saw nothing in the byre like oil or paraffin stored in drums, but the inspector's found pieces of some kind of metal, mebbe more than one. It's pretty certain that whatever was in these drums, or drum, was what caused the explosion, and mebbe the original fire too.'

Alex was frowning, though he made no verbal objection to the inference. 'Well, I think you'll have to look further afield for your arsonist, if that's what you have in mind, sergeant,' he told the man quietly. 'In fact Miss Francis has recently agreed to sell Hepburn's Quay to me, so she has absolutely nothing to gain by setting it on fire—quite the reverse. Family or not, I don't buy ruins.'

'Ah, well now.' The man rubbed the side of his nose thoughtfully, casting a shrewd glance between her and Alex. 'Then it's a mystery indeed, sir, is it not? For who else would want to do a thing like this?'

Alex shrugged and ran a hand through his hair. 'Who knows?' he said. 'Mebbe—tinkers, or a tramp making himself a kip for the night. Och, who knows?'

'Well, somebody does, sir, that's for sure,' the sergeant insisted. 'Those drums did not get there by themselves and it is unlikely that a tramp would be equipped with them, would you think?' He spoke to Alex, but something about Carla's manner had drawn his attention and he looked directly at her. 'Have you something in mind, Miss Francis?'

Carla hesitated, glancing briefly at Alex, then quickly away again, for she did have something in mind. She was remembering the McKinnons and their glowering looks of frustration when they left after that eventful visit, only the day before the fire. In describing his in-laws, Alex had described them as a tinker family, and he had suggested that the fire might have been started by tinkers. But how could she say that if she suspected anyone at all of deliberately setting fire to the old byre, it had to be his wife's parents?

'No,' she said in a small and slightly unsteady voice, 'no, I haven't anything in mind.'

CHAPTER SEVEN

CARLA had to admit to finding it much more pleasant having someone else get her breakfast for her. In fact she thought she could well get used to living at Hepburn's Carse and enjoy it, but she had no intention of weakening to the extent of moving in altogether as Annie wanted her to.

The Carse branch of the Hepburns had never been what could be termed wealthy, but descending from the elder one of the notorious Johnnie's sons they had always been just that bit better off than those at the Quay. They owned the bulk of the land, for one thing, while the branch that Carla came from merely had the house and a small piece of garden. Now that Alex had made such a success of his ranch-style farm, of course, it put them far ahead of anything they had known before.

A cook-housekeeper to relieve Annie of the more arduous duties, and a regular daily help, made life very comfortable, and it was a state of affairs that Carla found much to her liking. She was becoming thoroughly lazy, she feared, as she took her leave of Annie after breakfast and started out for her own less comfortable home. As she had done each day she had been there so far, she paused beside the paddock to look at the horses, and inevitably Alex put in an appearance before she had been there for more than a few seconds.

He always breakfasted much earlier than the rest of them did, so this meeting by the paddock was their first contact of the day and was surely too regular to be entirely accidental; at least it pleased her to think so.

As always she turned and smiled at him, experiencing a glowing sense of contentment at the sight of the familiar tanned features and warm brown eyes.

'Good morning.' He leaned beside her on the paddock fence and his bare arm touched hers, a light, deliberate contact that added warmth to her cheeks. 'Am I required to be ferryman this morning?'

It was a standing joke between them after several days of his taking her back and forth to the hospital to visit Tom, and she smiled as a matter of course, though it was as much a grimace as a smile this morning. 'I think not today, thank you,' she told him, and ran a fingertip along the fence rail. 'Mrs Laxey's back from Algeria to see him, and she wouldn't be at all pleased to find me there.' Catching the swift upward tilt of his brows, she hastened to correct any misconception. 'His mother,' she said. 'She doesn't approve of me.'

'Ah, I see.' He still watched her curiously, though Carla made no attempt to meet his eyes at the moment. 'But surely Tom will have some say in that, won't he?'

It was not an easy matter to discuss with Alex, and Carla shrugged, keeping her eyes on the horses still. 'It's probably for the best in the long run. Tom knows his mother's opinion of me, and I *have* been to see him every day so far.'

Alex's expression suggested he saw that as the obvious and natural thing to do, but he did not say so. Instead he changed the subject completely, and in doing so, took her by surprise and put her in a quandary wondering how to answer him. With his arms along the top rail and his chin resting on them, he too watched the quietly grazing animals while he spoke. 'Who do you suspect of starting the fire at the Quay?' he asked.

She turned swiftly and looked at him, catching only a sideways and deceptively lazy glance in response. 'Why—I don't know.'

'But you have some idea who it *might* be?' He frowned, impatience drawing at his reddish brows. 'Oh, come on, Carla, you obviously had ideas about it when Sergeant Muir was questioning you yesterday, even though you denied it. Who or what were you thinking of when you got that—guilty look so suddenly?'

'Guilty?' Carla straightened up and stood facing him, conscious as she always was when he was close to her, of just how tall he was. 'I don't have any reason to look guilty, *I* didn't start it, and I don't have any idea who did!'

With one arm along the fence top, Alex regarded her for a moment in silence, and she found it much too hard to face him in the circumstances. She thought it quite possible that the McKinnons had had something to do with starting the fire out of sheer malice, although she did not accept that they had done it with any intention of seeing Tom hurt. But she still could not bring herself to suggest it to Alex, no matter how contemptuous he was of his father-in-law.

'You're not a very good liar, hein.' He spoke softly and the effect of it sent a small shiver through her whole body. 'You thought of something or somebody, it was writ plain on your face. And it wasn't only me who noticed it, Rob Muir did too, and he'll not leave it there, he'll come back to it, you can take my word.'

'Then he'll be unlucky too!' She would have turned back to lean on the rail again, but Alex took her arm, then put his other hand under her chin and tilted her face up to him.

His eyes were narrowed and he looked at her in a way that made her tremble anxiously. 'What are you scared of, Carla?'

He still spoke quietly and the effect was more compelling because of it. 'I'm not frightened of anything,' she denied. 'Why should I be?'

He was frowning, and she wished he wouldn't, for it
made her feel quite unnecessarily guilty. 'I don't know,'
he confessed after a moment or two, 'I can only guess.
And that's what frightens *me*. I don't see you as an
arsonist, but the way you're behaving I'm beginning to
think I could be wrong; or that you at least know something about it.'

'Alex, for heaven's sake!' She stared at him in
mingled dismay and indignation. 'I—I wouldn't have
the nerve; and anyway, what reason would I have? I've
already agreed to sell the property to you, I'd only lose
a good sale by trying to burn the place down.' She
looked at him and shook her head slowly. 'I don't know
why you should think me as addle-pated as that, even
if you do have a pretty low opinion of me!'

Maybe it was simply by way of being an apology that
he bent his head suddenly and touched his mouth to
hers, but his nearness brought a trembling weakness to
her legs, and she would so willingly have exchanged
further discussion for the more passionate touch of his
lips. Instead he pressed on with his determined questioning.

'Then why did you look as you did, hein, eh?' He
studied her for a moment and she saw a look in his
eyes suddenly that suggested he was off on a new tack.
'What does Tom Laxey have to say about it?' he asked.
'He must have some thoughts on what started it,
surely.'

'I don't know.' She set her chin at a defiant angle,
but still felt rather a fool for having to tell him that
she had never once got around to questioning Tom
because she had never yet had the heart to. 'I—I
haven't asked him, and he hasn't said anything.'

Quite clearly Alex was finding it hard to believe; he
was frowning and his eyes sought her unwilling ones,
failed to do so, and once more raised her chin with his

hand. 'D'you tell me that you've seen the man every day since, and you've not once asked him what happened?' She shook her head and his tongue clicked impatiently. 'Damn it woman, why not?'

Carla jerked her head free, brushing away his hand as she did so. 'Because he wasn't well enough to be—be third-degreed,' she insisted. 'He's in pain, Alex; I couldn't sit there and demand to know what happened. It wasn't as if the house burned down, it was only an old byre!'

'So you just sat and held his hand like a wee angel of mercy!' Alex taunted, then almost at once reached for her hand and squeezed it tightly. 'No, I'm sorry, Carla, I shouldn't chide you for being soft-hearted, but Rob Muir'll have no such qualms, you know. He's on the track of those drums of something the expert found and he's bound to follow it up, sooner or later.'

'Only when the doctor allows him to,' Carla said. 'But Tom hasn't been fit to be questioned so far.' She challenged him with bright defiant eyes. 'He isn't your fire-raiser, anyway—it isn't Tom's style!'

'Then whose style is it?' They were back to the vexatious question of the McKinnons again, and she was still unwilling to tell him. But he gave her no more time to evade the issue and gripped both her arms with his strong fingers. 'Carla, will you stop havering, woman, and come clean? You've got some bee in your bonnet and I want to know what it is!'

Carla struggled to free herself, angry at being cornered and faced with the inevitable. 'All right, all right!' She rubbed her hands over the marks on her arms and swallowed hard. 'It was you who first put the idea into my head, when you suggested tinkers might have started the fire. I—I remembered you'd told me that the McKinnons were tinkers, or they were once, and they were furious with me for——'

'Aye, aye, I remember!'

She eyed him warily, half expecting an indignant denial, no matter what his feelings for his father-in-law were. But he said nothing more and she studied his face surreptitiously from the closeness of her lashes. Those fine lines at the corners of his eyes, and the firm set of his mouth. A strong passionate face that still disturbed her more than any other man ever had, and made her want to reach up and touch him; to try and coax a smile to those tight lips once more.

'I'm sorry,' she whispered.

'Why should you be?' Alex demanded swiftly. 'It's a feasible possibility, much as I dislike it, and, as you say, I put the idea into your head originally! I don't blame you, you've no need to be upset over it, at all.'

He turned and once more rested his arms along the top rail of the fence, so quiet and thoughtful that she felt strangely distant from him suddenly. But while she watched him, from the corner of her eye she caught a movement suddenly, and glanced across to see a car pulled up in front of the house, and a woman getting out.

Their conversation had scarcely been an enjoyable one, but there was always a certain sense of intimacy about being with Alex, and it was about to be brought to an end, she could count on it. So that she glared with unconscious malevolence at the tall, willowy figure of Caroline Millar.

She was the last person Carla wished to see at the moment, for she had never felt less like being sociable to a woman whom she frankly disliked. In the circumstances, since there was little possibility of them pursuing their present conversation further, Carla decided to leave, before Alex even realised they were about to be interrupted.

'There doesn't seem to be very much else we can say

at the moment, does there?' she said, and ignored the swift frown he turned on her, anxious only to be away before Caroline Millar joined them. She inclined her head in the direction of the tall blonde, already making her way across to the paddock with as much haste as she decently could without making it too obvious. 'You're going to have company,' she told him, 'and I have things to do, Alex.'

'Wait now!'

The fact that he would have detained her she took as a good sign, and could not resist making a gesture of some kind, now that the other woman was within hearing. 'I'll see you this evening as usual, Alex—'bye now!' Then, because she could not really ignore her altogether, much as she was tempted to, she gave Caroline Millar a brief nod and a half-smile as she turned to go. 'Good morning. Miss Millar!'

Obviously the visitor felt herself under no such obligation to be polite, for she made no gesture other than a slight lift of her brows and watched her go without even an acknowledging nod. Their dislike was mutual, but the other woman evidently saw no necessity to disguise it, as Carla herself did.

Annie had told her that Caroline Millar came over to Hepburn's Carse every day without fail, and no one was in any doubt as to why she came. With that fact in mind, Carla assumed that Alex was no less aware of it than anyone else, but he apparently did nothing to discourage the visits. That fact she resented bitterly, though without being fully aware that she did so.

Resolutely keeping her back turned, she made her way along the paddock fence, for she had no desire to see what kind of greeting Alex gave his visitor. She was so deeply engrossed in her own thoughts, in fact, that she scarcely noticed someone hurrying along behind her until she reached the open ground between the

Carse property and her own. A kind of no-man's-land that neither family had ever laid claim to.

She turned quickly and in some surprise when Colin came running up beside her, flushed and slightly out of breath, so that it was evident he had been trying to catch up with her. Having already seen him at breakfast, she frowned at him curiously, for it was clear he had some other reason in mind than simply keeping her company, or he would not have run so hard to catch up with her.

He fell into step beside her, giving her one of his rare and rather shy smiles. 'To what do I owe this pleasure?' she asked him lightly. 'Is something wrong, Col?'

He shook his head and shrugged. 'I just felt like talking.'

'Oh, I see.'

She left him to make the opening after that and was nothing loath to simply make her way in silence until he got around to it. It was the best part of the day, this cool morning silence, and she enjoyed the walk along the loch-side. The sun was still quite hazy, but promised a warm day later on, and the rich, earthy scents she enjoyed so much hung heavily in the air. It was a good place to be, and she once more thought of the delight of spending the rest of her life there, no matter how impracticable it was in view of her circumstances.

The heathery turf yielded to every step and added its own pungent scent to the morning, and the sun glinting on the tiny loch made it seem much larger than it was. Smooth and placid, its peat-brown waters just rippled over the stony shore and the tangled roots of scrub, making soft chuckling sounds, so that when Colin eventually spoke and broke the tranquillity of it all, she actually felt a moment of resentment.

'Carla, you're—pretty friendly with Alex, aren't you?' She turned swiftly and frowned at him. 'I mean, you get along with him,' Colin hastened to add.

'I suppose so,' she allowed cautiously, and once more frowned at his raw young profile, incredibly childish still in this soft morning light. 'What is it, Col? Is there anything I can help you with?'

He shrugged, taking a moment or two, presumably to assemble the right words. 'I wondered,' he said after several moments, 'whether he'd said anything to you about—well, about getting married again.'

'Good heavens, no!' She had denied it vehemently before she stopped to think that it wasn't quite true. But something in his manner made her quite inexplicably nervous, or perhaps anxious rather than nervous; whatever it was it gave her a sudden sickening sensation in her stomach and made her look at Colin warily. 'What's all this about, Colin?'

'Oh, I don't know!' He thrust both hands into his pockets and slouched along beside her untidily. Undoubtedly he had something on his mind that troubled him, and Carla felt sorry for him; it was hard to admit it, but Colin and his father seemed to have no shred of knowledge or understanding of one another. 'It was something Caroline said,' he went on after a moment or two. 'You know she always sides with anything and everything that Alex says and does, and she's never passed any opinion about whether or not she thinks I should be allowed to go to veterinary college.' He turned and looked at her with a steady directness very reminiscent of his father. 'Now she says she's on my side.'

Carla saw little danger in Caroline Millar professing her support to Colin himself, but she wondered what lay behind her being so frank with him. 'Why are you surprised, Colin?' She was not going to say too much yet, until she discovered the connection between Caroline Millar's sudden and unexpected support, and

Colin's mention of remarriage. 'Maybe she just thought you needed some encouragement.'

'It's more than that,' Colin insisted, striding along, shoulders slumped, and frowning as if the whole situation was beyond him. 'She spoke as if—well, as if she was going to be in a position to do something about it before too long, and I wondered—you know.'

'You think she has that much influence with Alex?' Carla asked, and did not really want to know the answer if it was the wrong one.

'I don't know.' He gazed at her frankly for a moment. 'I thought it was you had the pull with him,' he confessed. 'I hoped it was, but now—well, I don't know.'

'Wishful thinking?' Carla suggested, not without malice, and Colin made a face.

'Mebbe, but if Alex *does* marry her and she manages to get him to relent about me being a vet——'

'You're quite prepared to accept her as your step-mother!' Carla guessed bitterly. 'Oh, Colin, that's a very short-sighted view and completely self-centred!'

He gave her a swift sideways look from the corners of his eyes, a curiously sly look that just for a moment reminded her uncomfortably of his maternal grandfather. 'I'd rather it was you, of course, Carla,' he said, 'and mebbe if you could—talk to him. He's a great liking for you and you're much prettier than yon Caroline, mebbe if you put your mind to it, you could stop him from marrying her and change his mind about me at the same time. Would you try, Carla?'

Too staggered for the moment to take him quite seriously, Carla walked in silence. She had already tried to make Alex see things from Colin's point of view, and failed on each occasion, and she was definitely dubious about getting any more deeply involved, particularly since Caroline Millar seemed so confident of her own chances.

It stood to reason that if there was a chance of Caroline becoming the second Mrs Hepburn she would be glad to see her stepson sent off to college for several years. If he did follow his own inclinations and took no interest in the estate, then she might be thinking along the lines of her own offspring inheriting Hepburn's Carse, despite Alex's professed doubts about her in that direction.

'You could threaten to change your mind about letting him have the Quay, as a last resort,' Colin suggested, breathing temptation in her ear. 'You've got the whip-hand at the moment, for he's gey feared of losing it at this point.'

'Certainly not!' She spoke sharply, appalled by his ruthlessness until she realised he probably spoke only in bravado. Boylike and incredibly vulnerable despite his superior inches, he said whatever came into his head, and she shook her head when she looked at him, unable to resist a faint smile. 'That would be blackmail,' she told him, 'and I haven't come down to that yet.'

'You won't try to talk to him, then?'

His grey eyes were no longer sly, but appealing, just as they had been when he was the small boy she had so often amused on long summer days while his father was away. 'All right,' she said after a moment or two, and sighed deeply. 'But I warn you, it won't work, Col. Alex already knows my opinion, and he wasn't very pleased with me for expressing it; but—I'll try again.'

'Och, I knew you would!'

'But for your sake, not because I have any idea of ruining Caroline Millar's chance of becoming your stepmother, is that understood?'

Colin looked at her directly and with the same penetrating steadiness his father so often did. 'Och, aye,' he said, 'I understand.'

Carla had not long finished lunch when Alex arrived, and she looked up from pulling weeds to brush a forearm across her sticky brow, wondering what was so important that it would not keep until that evening when she went across to spend the night at the Carse. Surely Colin had not dangled that blackmail idea in front of him after all.

It was much better being outside, even though weeding the overgrown garden was hot and back-breaking work, and she was flushed and warm as she watched Alex coming along the path with his customary impatient stride. Stopping when he saw her, he did not even smile at the grimace she made when she straightened her back.

'I thought I'd better make a start on it,' she ventured by way of an opening, but he seemed too abstracted at the moment to do more than make a brief nod of agreement.

'Can I interrupt you for a few minutes?' he asked, and Carla gazed at him for a moment searchingly. Then dropping the trowel she held on to the ground, she led the way into the house. They faced each other across the table and Carla was still wary more than curious, because she thought she knew what he was there for. 'I've been to see the McKinnons.' Catching her startled eye, he went on, 'They were moving house this morning, so it was an opportunity to go without arousing their curiosity too much. Although I'm not in the habit of paying social calls on my in-laws,' he added with a tight smile.

'You—you didn't say anything about——'

'Not openly, of course not.' He interrupted her hastily, almost as if he feared to hear her mention her suspicion aloud. 'They assumed I'd come to make sure they actually went, as they were supposed to.'

'You found them the cottage they've moved to, of

course, didn't you? That was good of you, in the circumstances.'

'Oh, but I had an ulterior motive, surely they mentioned that when they were here, didn't they?' One glance at her face was sufficient to confirm it, and once more that tight, humourless smile tugged at his wide mouth. 'I admit it—I want them as far away from Colin as possible, although they'll still see him, and I can't stop them, of course, in all fairness. He *is* their grandson, though I wish to God he wasn't!'

'Alex!'

He frowned, shaking his head impatiently. 'Water under the bridge,' he quoted. 'As for the other matter, I skated round it without coming out and accusing them, as I'd like to have done, but I have to admit I'm no wiser. All I learned was that they were disappointed it wasn't the Carse that was burned instead, though they were quite satisfied to know it was all in the family.'

Carla could not quite feel so intensely as he did about them, but she could well imagine what a thorn in his flesh the McKinnons had been all those years. She understood perfectly his need to get his son as far away from them as possible, but she hoped Colin would not eventually be driven to visiting them more and more often and let himself be influenced against his father. With the situation as it was between Colin and Alex it would be all too easy to make the breach a permanent one, and she would hate for that to happen, even though it might suit Caroline Millar better.

'What can we do about—that other matter?' she asked, and Alex shrugged.

'God knows—I should mention it to Rob Muir, I suppose.'

'Oh, Alex, must you?' She was caught up in that dark, unfathomable gaze and shivered slightly without being sure why. 'I mean, they're Colin's grandparents, whatever they are and whatever they've done. I wouldn't like to think of him being hurt because he knows you—we suspect them. It was only a byre, after all, it isn't as if I shall be claiming compensation or anything like that. Must he know, Alex?'

He got up and walked across to the window, gazing out across the overgrown garden to the pier and the loch beyond that; perhaps trying to still the turbulent emotions that raged in him with the tranquillity of the scene outside. She could only guess at what was going on in his mind as she watched him in silence.

'He already knows.' He spoke as if he regretted it more than he had ever regretted anything in his life, and she could believe he did. He half-turned, hands thrust into his pockets. 'He overheard me talking to Grandmother about it; he heard her agree it was quite possible they had a hand in it, and——' There was something infinitely appealing in the helpless shrug of broad shoulders, and Carla caught her lip between her teeth. 'He was upset, to put it mildly. Not that he holds much brief for them, but they *are* his grandparents and he has something of them in his make-up. He possibly understands them having a motive for doing something like that, much better than we can.'

'Poor Colin!'

'Aye, poor Colin.' He turned right round from the window and looked at her for a moment with his strong features softened by shadows, and his brown eyes too deeply unreadable to tell her anything. 'He goes to see them, did you know?' She nodded without speaking, suspecting that all he needed was a willing ear, and he went on. 'It's simply because they know I want him to follow me and take over the Carse eventually that they've been urging him on to this vet business, among other things.'

Carla was reminded of her own promise to Colin earlier in the day, and she swallowed hastily before she pointed out her own feelings in that direction. 'I've always supported him in that too,' she reminded him, her voice strangely husky. 'So I gather, does Miss Millar.'

That last had been irresistible but from the way Alex looked it seemed he did not believe it. 'Who told you so?' he asked.

'Colin—this morning. He says she——'

'Oh, he reads whatever suits him best into whatever's said to him on that subject,' Alex interrupted shortly. 'Caroline has more sense than to encourage him, she knows my feelings in the matter.'

'And because she agrees with you that automatically makes her more sensible than me, of course!' snapped Carla, roused suddenly from sympathy to defiance by his stubbornness where Colin was concerned, and annoyed that he had so readily defended Caroline Millar. 'Why are you so—so—pig-headed about it, Alex? Is it such an awful thing to want to become a vet?'

She noticed how his mouth tightened and how the knuckles of the hand resting on a chair back showed the whiteness of bone through the tanned skin. 'You've asked me that before, on more than one occasion,' he reminded her, 'and you know *why* I feel as I do about it.'

'I know you won't listen to *Colin's* feelings about it!'

Her voice shook uncontrollably, however much she sought to control it, and she unconsciously took a half-step backwards when he came across the room towards her, then leaned over the table, resting his hands on it while he brought his face close to hers.

'You'll not give up, will you?' he said, and she screwed up her courage so as not to let Colin down.

'I just wish you'd see Colin's point of view, that's all.

I know how you've worked to build up the estate for him, Alex, but if——'

'It never fails, does it?' Alex demanded of the empty room, and threw out his hands in despair. 'You and Colin between you, you see me as a real tyrant, do you not?'

Appalled at being so misread, Carla shook her head urgently. Oh no, of course I don't, Alex, it's just that——'

'Jings, woman, you as good as just said so!' He glared at her furiously. 'Well, be damned to the pair of you! Mebbe I'll let him have his way and do his animal doctoring, seeing he sets such store by it, and you too, it seems!'

Carla's eyes widened hopefully. 'Oh, Alex, you——'

'Aye, and mebbe I'll get myself another son to leave all this to—I'm still man enough for that!'

Carla stared at him, her lips parted, and she jumped nervously when he turned and went striding out of the house, slamming the door hard behind him. Colin had got his way, or so she thought, but she wished she knew how much Caroline Millar had influenced the change of mind.

Too many things fitted together too neatly. Like Caroline Millar being so confident when she talked to Colin, and then Alex yielding after so long on something he felt very strongly about. Combined with Alex's furious declaration about having more sons to inherit his precious land they added up to a very discomfiting possibility, and Carla brushed an impatient hand across her eyes as she walked outside once more. She had told Colin that she despised the kind of blackmail he suggested, but at the moment she had to admit to being very tempted.

CHAPTER EIGHT

CARLA needed to do some shopping in Gibbert the following morning, but after a great deal of thought, she decided against asking Alex to take her in. After seeing the angry, emotional mood he had left in the previous day she was disinclined to face another meeting so soon, and particularly a drive in to Gibbert. So instead she telephoned for a taxi to fetch her, making sure that Annie did not overhear the call and scold her for it. It was one of the times when she wished she could drive and had a car of her own; and one of the very few times she regretted being so far from what Tom called civilisation.

Gibbert wasn't very big, but it had all the necessary shops as well as a couple of quite good restaurants, that mostly catered for passing coach traffic. Carla thought it was the first time she had gone there alone and she missed Tom's company as she walked around the shops, wondering how much longer the much travelled Mrs Laxey would be staying.

Tom saw little of his mother, in fact, but she still kept an interested eye on his activities and vetted all his girl-friends, deciding on their suitability or otherwise. Carla had definitely come under the heading of unsuitable, but just how firmly Tom would have stuck to his right to choose when it came to the point, Carla could never really be sure.

Having finished her shopping, she made her way to a rather good little coffee-shop in the centre of town; somewhere she had gone a couple of times with Tom. Sitting at one of the small tables, she deposited her

shopping on another chair and looked around her. It
was a second or two before she recognised a familiar
face, newly arrived at the next table, and seeing Caroline Millar added nothing to her enjoyment.

Normally hers was a friendly and out-going nature
and she would have greeted someone she knew unhesitatingly, but Caroline Millar was a different proposition. The woman seated herself with an effortless
grace it was impossible not to envy, but shook her head
at the waitress's request for an order and lit a cigarette
instead. It was when she raised her head from the
lighter-flame that she noticed Carla, and some kind of
recognition became inevitable.

'Good morning, Miss Millar.'

Carla spoke first, risking the expected snub. But
quite unexpectedly her greeting was not only acknowledged but accompanied by a rather tentative smile.
'You're not waiting for someone, are you?' Caroline
asked.

Surprised at even being acknowledged, Carla shook
her head. There was, she thought, a suggestion of
anxiety in the question and it puzzled her. 'No,' she
said, 'I'm not expecting anyone.'

'Ah!' Apparently the reply afforded some satisfaction, and for a moment white teeth gleamed between
red lips. 'I *am*!' The smile was frankly smug. 'You
haven't seen Alex heading this way, have you?'

Bitchiness was not normally one of Carla's vices, but
just for a moment she was very tempted to linger long
enough over her coffee for Alex to arrive, and then ask
for a lift home. Caroline Millar brought out the very
worst in her, she feared. The temptation lasted for only
a moment, however, then she shook her head.

'Sorry,' she said, 'I haven't seen him at all this morning.' Then because it was irresistible, she added, 'Is he
keeping you waiting?'

The smile that greeted the suggestion had an edge like a sword, but still she attempted a knowingly coy look that Carla found hard to swallow in the circumstances. 'Oh no,' Caroline assured her sweetly, 'Alex *never* keeps me waiting, but—well, you probably know how it is with your own boy-friend, it always *seems* such a long time since you last saw him.'

'Oh, I'm sure it does!'

Carla found it incredibly difficult being even normally civil to her, and because she was not anxious to prolong a very discomfiting situation, she drank her coffee as quickly as possible. Perversely, Caroline seemed bent on making conversation, a complete reversal of her normal behaviour and not without a good reason, Carla suspected.

The tables were close enough to make it possible to carry on a conversation without the necessity of raising their voices, and Caroline leaned an elbow on the table and waxed confidential. 'You don't really *know* Alex very well, do you?' she asked, and Carla blinked for a moment uncomprehendingly, wondering where this was leading. 'I mean,' Caroline went on, 'I know you're some kind of distant cousin, but you haven't really seen all that much of him over the years, have you?'

Carla was reluctant to admit it, but she supposed she did not really know Alex as well as she had always supposed she did. That fact had been brought home to her once or twice lately when she had learned various things about him that she had never dreamed could be true. Just the same, she did not readily admit the truth to Caroline Millar.

'I suppose not,' she allowed. 'Although, as you say, we are both family.'

'Oh yes—family!' The bright red mouth showed a distinct sneer for a second, but apparently the closeness of the Hepburns was not the axe she was grinding at

the moment, and Carla wondered just what she *was*
leading up to. 'Did you ever see Alex's first wife?'

Taken by surprise, Carla eyed her warily for a
moment. His *first* wife, she noted; as if Caroline was in
no doubt that there was going to be a second Mrs Alex
Hepburn, or who was going to fill the role.

More than likely Alex would find it less easy to speak
of Isabella to her, for he was astute enough to realise
Caroline would be a much less sympathetic listener
than Carla had been. And to Carla there was a curious
satisfaction in that. But she disliked this conversation
altogether, and prayed it was not going to lead to her
hearing confirmation of Alex's plans to remarry.

'I saw Isabella a couple of times,' she admitted, and
Caroline pounced quickly, blue eyes gleaming.

'What was she like?'

Was she simply probing for the sake of it, Carla
wondered, or did she have some definite motive in
mind? Whatever the reason, Carla felt obliged to give
poor misguided Isabella her due. 'She was very pretty,
as far as I remember, but of course I was only seven or
eight at the time, and I don't honestly remember. Alex
says she was; very pretty.' That last had been irresistible, and she made no apology for it.

'Well, naturally!' Smoke issued in a stream from
pursed lips, and a gleaming look in her eyes left Carla
in no doubt that the opinion was resented. 'But it
would never have worked out, of course, if she'd lived.
I mean, how could it? A girl with her background just
wouldn't—fit in.'

Whatever she believed in her heart about Isabella's
suitability, Carla had no intention of discussing her
with Caroline Millar, and she did not hesitate to let her
know it. 'I'm hardly qualified to pass an opinion,' she
said. 'And I'd much rather not discuss Alex's private
business.'

'Oh, come on!' Caroline taunted. 'Don't tell me *you* hold any brief for the McKinnon clan—not after the trouble you've had with them lately!'

For a moment Carla was too stunned to reply. The last thing she expected was for Alex to have spoken to anyone outside the immediate family about their suspicions regarding the McKinnons. It could only mean, she thought, that if he had told Caroline Millar, then their relationship was every bit as advanced as Colin had suggested.

Summoning every ounce of self-control, Carla shrugged with assumed nonchalance. 'We don't know that they had anything to do with starting the fire, it's only a—a guess. We hope for Colin's sake it isn't true. Alex is right to hesitate; they *are* Colin's grandparents, after all.'

Caroline's blue and slightly tip-tilted eyes were shadowed by heavy lids, but just for a moment Carla would have sworn that they betrayed surprise. The impression was short-lived, however, and she was smiling again, but in such a way that little icy trickles shivered along Carla's back. 'Oh, but fire-raising isn't something that can be overlooked,' Caroline insisted. 'Relations or not, I for one shall *insist* that Alex take his suspicions, however nebulous, to the police. That, I think, would dispose of the McKinnon problem once and for all!'

She would insist. Carla swallowed the fact that she was so confident Alex would do as she said, and gave her a glance from her green eyes that would have been heeded by anyone less sure of herself than Caroline Millar. 'The decision will eventually be mine, I imagine,' Carla told her, and for a moment met that confident blue gaze head on. 'Hepburn's Quay still belongs to me, in fact, Miss Millar.'

She swallowed the rest of her coffee thankfully. Crossing swords with Caroline Millar was much more nerve-shattering than fighting with Alex, and not nearly as enjoyable. Nevertheless the other woman's unmistakable surprise gave her a moment's satisfaction. Presumably that was something Alex had *not* confided to her.

'But you have agreed to sell?' Caroline insisted. 'And you won't break your word to Alex; I know you!'

'On the contrary!' Carla collected her bill and her shopping and glanced only briefly at the next table before she moved away. 'If I do happen to bump into Alex, I'll tell him you're still waiting,' she said. 'Good-bye, Miss Millar!'

In fact she bumped into Alex almost literally, in the doorway of the coffee-house, and she despaired of the sudden urgent thudding of her heart when his strong fingers gripped her arms to prevent a more violent collision. Instinctively she was tempted to laugh and make a joke of the situation, but knowing that Caroline Millar was sitting there waiting for him hardened her heart. Instead she pulled free of him, but dropped her shopping bag in the process and scattered groceries everywhere.

Crouched beside her on the tiled entrance porch, Alex helped her gather them up. 'Will you come and have coffee with me?' he asked when they were once more upright, and Carla's gaze went automatically to the tall willowy figure supported by her elbows and looking bored.

'No, thank you,' she told him. 'I've already had mine.'

It was hard to stand so near to him and not remember the sensation of being in his arms, and how wildly exciting that firm straight mouth could be when he kissed her. Seeing Caroline Millar there stiffened her resistance, but it didn't make her immune to his heavy-lidded gaze.

'You're getting back at me for yesterday, is that it?' She did not answer, and a big brown hand reached down for her free one, grasping it firmly and hanging on. 'Come on, Carla; is that why you're looking so po-faced and keeping your distance? What do you want me to say? That I'm sorry I went off the deep end like I did?'

By now Carla felt sure they would be under observation by those sharp blue eyes, and she shook her head. The deliberately hard pressure of his fingers gave her a strangely breathless feeling that showed in her voice. 'You don't have to say anything about yesterday,' she denied, but realised she might just as well not have spoken for all the notice he took.

'O.K., if that's what it takes to make you smile, then I'll say I'm sorry I slammed the door behind me and went off in high dudgeon!' He squeezed her fingers so hard that she almost cried out. 'Now smile at me, damn you!'

Carla managed it, just. Trying to break his hold, however, was as difficult as ever. 'Alex, will you please let go my hand, I have to go and find a taxi to take me home.'

Still holding on, he looked down at her and his brown eyes gleamed with some expression she could not properly define because she dared not look at him for long enough. 'Come and sit with me while I have my coffee and *I'll* run you home,' he insisted. 'You *must* have had it in for me this morning to call a taxi instead of asking me. Come on, hein, wait for me.' His voice was alarmingly persuasive, and she wavered.

'No, thank you!' She managed at last to free her hand, then inclined her head in the direction of the glass doors behind him. 'You don't need my company, you've someone waiting for you. Goodbye, Alex.'

Instinctively he turned and glanced through the

glass doors, and at the same moment Caroline Millar
caught his eye. She waved a hand and smiled, and by
the time Alex turned back, Carla was gone, ducking
and dodging the people who crowded the pavement
and putting as much distance as she could between
them.

It wasn't a hot day, but as she made her way along
Gibbert's main street Carla's face was burning. She had
neither right nor reason to feel so furiously angry about
the likelihood of Caroline Millar becoming Alex's
second wife, she told herself. His affairs were no concern of hers, and it was quite natural for a man to discuss family matters with the woman he was to marry.

Nevertheless as she went in search of a taxi to take
her home, she toyed once more with the idea of following Colin's suggestion. She was so very tempted to with-
hold the sale of Hepburn's Quay; not for the reason
Colin had suggested, but from sheer malice inspired by
her dislike of Caroline Millar.

'Idiot!' she told herself as she crossed over the busy
street; but she knew Caroline had been right—she
couldn't break her word to Alex.

A rather garbled message the previous evening had informed Carla that the coast was clear and would she
please go and see Tom. From which she gathered that
Mrs Laxey, having satisfied herself that her son was on
the road to recovery, had left Scotland and returned to
her African travels.

It was no use asking Alex to take her in to Gibbert
because she knew he had an appointment to view a replacement for the late lamented Grey, at a farm some
distance further afield than Gibbert, and in the other
direction. So instead she once more took a taxi, thinking to herself as the vehicle dipped and swerved on the
long road to Gibbert that she had never behaved so

extravagantly in her life as she had these past few days. At this rate her grandfather's legacy was not going to last very long.

One of the first things she discovered when she arrived at the hospital was that she had been mistaken about Tom's mother having gone back to her holiday. Her absence was only temporary, it seemed, and Carla was not altogether reassured by Tom's insistence that they had plenty of time to enjoy each other's company without interruption.

He looked so much improved since her last visit that she found it hard to believe he had lain there so vague and unresponsive only a matter of days before. He welcomed her with outstretched arms and kissed her long and hard when she got within reach, so that she drew back hastily the moment he released her. Not that she escaped altogether, for he retained his hold on one of her hands, and she was amazed at how much strength he had for a man who had been so ill such a short time ago.

'I've missed you,' he whispered, and held on to her hand so tightly that Carla had little option but to sit on the edge of the bed beside him.

He had been moved since her last visit, out of the public ward and into a small private ward that gave them complete privacy. At the instigation of his mother, she assumed, although obviously it suited Tom better to have her to himself, instead of being under observation in the bigger ward.

She felt oddly strange with him at the moment, and wished she had not submitted so readily to that warm welcoming kiss. For Tom to get the wrong idea about her concern for him was the last thing she wanted, and almost she regretted responding to his message so unhesitatingly.

'You're a lot better than when I saw you last,' she

told him. 'I'm glad you've recovered so quickly, now I needn't feel so guilty about you.'

'Guilty?' He quizzed her good-humouredly. 'You, my love? Why?'

Carla shrugged uneasily, hoping to keep the conversation on a casual, friendly level. 'Well, if it hadn't been for me you wouldn't have come to Scotland in the first place, and this wouldn't have happened. I've been waiting to hear your version of how it all started, Tom, but I didn't like to question you when you were so obviously poorly. Apparently it isn't as straightforward as it might be; I've had a policeman to see me and he'll be coming to see you as well, as soon as you're fit enough.'

Tom pulled a face. 'Sergeant R-R-Robert Muir-r-r?' he guessed, the grimace apologising for his exaggerated version of the sergeant's Scottish accent. 'He's been to see *me* too, love. In fact he left only just before you arrived; I couldn't put it off any longer.'

'Then he's told you about the drums the expert found in the byre?' Carla said. 'Tom, they think someone deliberately set the fire; or so it seems to me. I just don't know what to make of it.'

He squeezed her fingers tightly and he looked very much as if he only half-believed her confession of ignorance. 'They know all about it now, sweet, and the good sergeant is convinced it's no more than should be expected from a batty Sassenach. The truth is I've been putting off confessing my sins to the cops as long as possible, darling, but I must admit that I feel better now that I've done it.'

Carla was looking at him blankly, trying to imagine what on earth he had confessed to Sergeant Muir. She could not believe that he had set fire to the byre deliberately; that was out of the question, but perhaps he had been careless with a cigarette, and——

'Confession may be good for the soul,' Tom added, cutting into her silent speculation, 'but it doesn't do much for one's ego having to confess to having been a ruddy fool.'

She shook her head, gazing at him anxiously. 'Tom, I won't believe you're an arsonist, so I simply don't understand what you're trying to say.'

'Why, that the whole blessed conflagration was more or less my own fault,' Tom told her. 'You see, it comes of trying to fit a townie like me into your country scene. I'm not used to being miles from the nearest garage and I felt better with a hoard of petrol close at hand in the old byre. Safe as houses, I thought, but it only needed a—a careless flick of cigarette ash—which only goes to show how wrong I can be! As a matter of fact, I thought you might have had an inkling.'

Carla stared at him, blinking in disbelief. 'You—you mean you had petrol stored out there? Drums of petrol?'

'That's about the size of it, darling. I've made a full confession and explained that although the guy at the garage let me have the empty drums, I didn't tell him what I wanted them for. So he's in the clear.'

Carla was still finding it hard to believe that anyone as intelligent and astute as she knew Tom to be could behave with such criminal foolishness. She thought how she and Alex had discussed the possibility of the McKinnons being the culprits, and how upset Alex said Colin was when he overheard it discussed, and she shook her head despairingly.

'Oh, Tom, of all the—the stupid, dangerous things to do!'

'I *know*, I *know*!'

'You could have been killed!'

He pulled a face. 'I knew that too, and if it hadn't

been for your strong silent cousin, I probably would have been.'

'Alex?' Carla's heart lurched sickeningly, and almost certainly Tom felt the increased urgency of her pulse as he held her hand. 'Alex sent me to phone for the fire brigade while he drove over to see what he could do,' she recalled, speaking to remind herself as much as to Tom. 'I didn't go back to the Quay until it was all over, and no one said anything about—— You were inside when it happened?'

Tom nodded. 'One minute it was no more than smouldering straw, and the next——' He used his hands to illustrate his meaning, and Carla shivered. 'I remember lying there in the doorway of the byre wondering what had hit me, after that first blessed drum exploded, then your cousin Alex was pulling some dirty great beams off me and pulling me out, rolling me in something. After that——' He spread his hands resignedly, but it was clear that he appreciated what Alex had done for him, and for once his blue eyes were sober and serious. 'I'd like to thank him; if he isn't too intent on knocking my head off,' he added.

There was a half-scared look in Carla's eyes when she visualised the scene in the old yard at the back of Hepburn's Quay, and Alex had never even hinted at what had happened. Tom was eyeing her curiously, taking her hand again and drawing her closer. 'Didn't he say anything about it?' he asked, and she shook her head.

'And neither did you until now. I—I'd no idea he'd risked his life.'

It was almost an accusation, and Tom regarded her for a moment before he replied. 'I was feeling very fuzzy-headed, darling, I'd remind you. And anyway——' He paused, toying with her fingers and looking at them rather than at her face. 'Anyway I wasn't going to do anything to boost Alex Hepburn's stock with you. He's doing well enough in that direction without a public relations job by me!'

'And yet you've told me now,' Carla reminded him.

Her mind was still conjuring up pictures of Alex risking his neck to get Tom out of danger before the whole building collapsed on top of the pair of them, and she shivered again, quite involuntarily. It was as if Tom knew what was going on in her mind, for his mouth curved in a faint and almost bitter smile while he watched her.

'Maybe because I've finally seen the light, angel, and I *know* you won't marry me, if I keep after you for the next twenty years!' He looked up and gave her a glimpse of the more familiar smile for a moment. 'I've finally recognised that I haven't a snowball's chance in hell of getting you to fall in love with me. For the second time today my ego has taken a pounding, and it isn't easy to accept.'

It was a tricky moment, as Carla saw it. If she showed too much sympathy it might just give Tom reason to believe he was wrong about him having no chance, and yet she did genuinely regret that things couldn't have been different between them. She liked Tom, she always had, she was even fond of him, but she didn't love him and she could not do anything about that.

'I'm sorry, Tom.'

There seemed so little else to say at the moment, and Tom merely shook his head slowly. 'I'll have some charges to answer as soon as I'm on my feet again,' he guessed. 'Storing petrol illegally, for a start, but when it's all over, my redoubtable ma has a schedule all lined up for me. I shall take off for the sunny Greek isles and bask in the sun for a few weeks to restore my ego. Hot sun and golden sands are much more my scene than the hills and heather bit, you know, darling, as I've said before.'

'Yes, I know.' It was odd how sad she felt suddenly, as if something very special was coming to an end; as she supposed it was. 'Oh well,' she said, determinedly light, 'at least your mother will be pleased I'm out of the running.'

'*Damn* Ma! I'd have married you if the whole world objected, if you'd have had me!' He took both her hands this time and his fingers were tight about her wrists; his eyes more serious than she had ever seen and unexpectedly vulnerable too. 'I'm sorry it didn't work out, Carla; not just you and me, but the hotel business as well; it could have been fun even though I don't fit in up here—not like your Alex.'

The same fluttering urgency touched her pulse again, and Carla drew away her hands, folding them tightly together instead. 'He isn't *my* Alex,' she insisted. 'As far as I can gather, he's Caroline Millar's.'

Tom smiled and reached up to stroke her cheek with a gentle fingertip. 'How about me putting on the charm and luring her away from him?' he suggested, and Carla found herself smiling too.

'You've been dying to do that ever since you saw her with him in Gibbert,' she accused. 'You could probably do it too, and enjoy yourself at the same time!'

'I might.'

His eyes, she noticed, were still dark and serious and held no glimmer of laughter at all. He reached up his hands, curved invitingly, and she bent over him. Gently he cupped her face between them and gazed at her for a moment before drawing her down to him to kiss her mouth; a long, lingering kiss that was too gentle to convey passion, but which stirred her emotions until she felt like crying.

'My love,' he whispered softly.

Carla was vaguely aware of footsteps outside in the corridor, and she put her hands to Tom's wrists, turning her face to the door to listen. There was a gleam of resentment in Tom's eyes when he recognised his mother's voice, and Carla was already on her feet. Mrs Laxey was the last person she wanted to meet at this particular moment.

'I'll go,' she whispered to Tom, and he tried to reach her hand again, but she was already on her way to the door. Turning, she looked back for a moment. 'Goodbye, Tom.'

'You won't come and see me again?'

She half-turned her head to listen to the young nurse trying to dissuade Tom's mother from joining them, and smiled ruefully. 'If I get the opportunity,' she promised. 'Goodbye, Tom.'

As she opened the door into the corridor the smell of hospital soap and disinfectant was for the moment overpowered by an expensive French perfume, and Carla thanked heaven that just for the moment the nurse had prevailed upon the tall, elegant visitor to accompany her to the Sister's office. Maybe, she thought, it would save a lot of uncomfortable moments if Mrs Laxey did stay around for a while.

Carla supposed it was habit that made her linger beside the paddock the following morning; she could hardly expect Alex to come and join her as he usually did, after the way she had snubbed him last time. But in fact she saw him come walking down from the direction of the stables after only a few minutes, and she could do nothing about the sudden lightness of her heart.

Obviously he had something on his mind, for he walked with his hands thrust deep into the pockets of a pair of serviceable blue denims and with his head down. It almost seemed as if he might be unaware of her, but then he veered across towards the paddock as he habitually did, and leaned his arms along the top rail while he gave her a brief nod of greeting.

'Good morning.'

'Good morning, Alex.' She studied his serious face for a moment before venturing a question. 'Is there something wrong?'

'Wrong?' He turned his head, and brown eyes scanned her face for a moment. 'Not as far as I know,' he said. 'You seem prepared to speak to me this morning, I'm not being treated as if I have some ghastly disease; so I'd say everything's O.K.—thanks.'

'Oh, Alex!' He had resumed his stern profile stance, and she looked at him in mingled reproach and exasperation. 'You know what she'd have thought if I'd gone back in there with you—and in the circumstances I couldn't have blamed her.'

'By her you mean Caroline, I presume?' he guessed, and she nodded. 'You jump to a hell of a lot of conclusions, Carla, don't you? I gather in this instance that you thought Caroline was waiting for me?' She nodded, blaming him for not being able to see the awkwardness of the situation. 'Good grief, child, I always use that place when I'm in town! I wait for you in there when I take you to see your Tom. Caroline knows it as well as you should have done!'

Carla resented that 'child' bitterly, and she glared at him reproachfully. 'Well, I *didn't*! And she told me she was waiting for you, I was in no position to argue with her. Naturally in the circumstances, I——'

'In the circumstances you decided you didn't want to play gooseberry, and preferred a strategic withdrawal!' His mockery hurt as well as angered her, and her silence was confirmation enough that he had judged the situation correctly. 'So you gave me the cold shoulder and stalked off in virtuous indignation!' He turned and looked at her at last, and something in his expression brought swift colour to her cheeks. 'And there I was flattering myself that you might be jealous, when all the time you were simply leaving the coast clear!'

'Stop it, Alex!'

The brown eyes travelled slowly over her bright, angry face, and he shook his head. 'Too near home?' he suggested softly.

Hands clenched tightly into fists on the fence in front of her, Carla fought hard for self-control. It wasn't like the Alex she had always thought she knew to be cruel, and this she saw as a deliberate attempt to embarrass her by teasing her about her schoolgirl fancy for him.

'Too far from the truth!' she retorted in self-defence. 'I've outgrown that childish crush I had on you long ago!' Poking one toe through the bars of the fence, she examined it carefully. 'You're embarrassing me, Alex, and it isn't to your credit that you seem to be enjoying it. I wish you'd change the subject.'

Silence followed and she could sense some aura of emotion surrounding him, but after a second or two he nodded, and rather surprisingly complied. 'The police have been to see the McKinnons, did you know that? Did Grandmother tell you?' Carla shook her head, her pulse hammering anxiously, and he went on. 'I saw Blane McKinnon when I was riding over on the north moor yesterday, and he started yammering about it the minute I got within hearing. He was evidently on his way over to us to make a row about it; luckily I forestalled him.'

'You—you told the police after all?'

'I did not.' Alex turned and looked at her again, his brows drawn. 'He told me Rob Muir had called on them the day before yesterday. He'd told them there'd been a phone call from a woman, suggesting that the McKinnons knew something about the fire, and of course Muir's familiar enough with them to take anything into account.' For just a moment his frown was relieved by a faint smile. 'I don't think I've ever seen Blane McKinnon so full of outraged dignity in my life. He immediately thought it was me, of course, until he was told the call came from a woman, then he decided it must be you.'

'Did Sergeant Muir say who she was?'

Alex shrugged, his eyes regarding her curiously. 'Apparently the lady preferred to remain anonymous; but I must admit, I thought it must be you.'

'Oh, Alex!'

'It *wasn't* you?'

Her cheeks flushed, she angled her chin. 'I don't make anonymous calls, and you surely don't think I'd mention this without saying anything to you,' she objected.

He was obviously not so sure as she expected him to be. 'I don't know,' he demurred. 'You weren't exactly my greatest fan when we last saw one another, and you could have decided to act off your own bat.'

'Well, I didn't!' She only just stopped herself from reminding him that Caroline Millar also knew about their suspicions. 'Anyway,' she said, 'it doesn't matter much now that Tom's told Sergeant Muir all about it.'

Alex was frowning at her again and it was clear that he expected her to explain. In the circumstances she supposed he was entitled to know, but she did not relish relating how stupidly Tom had behaved. Eventually she made the facts known to him as briefly as possible, and saw the fierce darkness in his eyes well before she finished.

'Of all the damned idiots!' he declared. 'And he's supposed to be an intelligent man, presumably! Och, how can anyone be so daft as to put drums of petrol among straw in an old byre?' He took no notice of her half-hearted protests, but regarded her thoughtfully for a minute. 'When did he tell Muir about this, do you know?'

Carla shrugged. 'Just before I got there, he said. Yesterday afternoon.'

'Oh, what perfect timing!' Alex shook his head slowly and looked down at his feet. 'Why in heaven's name didn't he speak up sooner?'

'Because he was too ill to talk to the police, and because——' She shrugged uneasily, suspecting the second reason was the more likely one. 'Well, because he knew he'd been stupid and he didn't like having to admit it. He didn't say anything until he had to.'

'Until it was too late, damn him!' Alex swore.

Eyeing him curiously, Carla tried to guess what he was talking about. 'What do you mean, too late? Too late for what, Alex?'

He explained carefully, as if he was telling a slightly backward child, and took not the slightest notice of her bright flush of resentment. 'The McKinnons know that it was you who gave their name to the police, and——'

'But I told you, I didn't, Alex!'

'Then who did?' Alex demanded. 'Grandmother would have given her name, and anyway she's too much care for Col's feelings to have tried to have the McKinnons blamed, even though she was convinced they were responsible.'

'And you think I'm less—less sensitive to your son's feelings, is that it?'

Her voice was husky and very unsteady, and she realised with alarm that she felt horribly like crying because he was so ready to believe she had informed against the McKinnons, Colin's grandparents. But it seemed as if he sensed how she felt and after a moment's

silence he looked at her with a curiously anxious look
in his eyes.

'I think mebbe it didn't occur to you,' he began, but
she jumped in quickly, determined to convince him.

'Alex, I *didn't* tell them!'

She was angry and hurt, and she had never been
more anxious for his support. Mostly it hurt because
he apparently did not even consider Caroline as an
alternative to herself where informing the police was
concerned, and she could almost hate him for that.
Nevertheless she was not going to suggest it; not for
anything would she give him reason to suspect she
hated the very idea of Caroline Millar becoming his
wife.

'What happens now?' she asked, in a small flat voice.

The firm line of his mouth tightened noticeably, and
his hands on the paddock rail looked taut and hard.
'What happens now is that the McKinnons get the—
just what they're asking as compensation for their injured pride. Laxey's belated confession is all they need
as a stick to beat us with!'

Carla stared at him. This was a new element, and an
infinitely disturbing one, and it made her see that she
had not until now taken the whole business of the
McKinnons seriously enough. 'Alex, they're not—
they're not suing for—libel, or whatever it is?'

He laughed shortly, but the burning fierceness in
his eyes allowed no suggestion of humour. 'Are you
willing to take the chance?' he demanded. 'Slander is a
nasty business and it has a habit of sticking. In this case
there's too much likelihood of it being true for the
rumour to be easily quashed, and that means the
McKinnons have a pretty good case now that your
friend has piped up at the eleventh hour with his confession!'

It was very difficult to think clearly at the moment,

and Carla looked at him helplessly. 'Alex, what am I going to do?'

'Nothing,' Alex told her firmly. 'You're going to do nothing, just sit tight and leave everything to me.'

'But you said something about compensation. How much are they asking for? I have Grampy's money——'

'I said leave everything to me,' Alex interrupted shortly, and something about the sudden evasiveness of his eyes puzzled her.

'You're not——' The light dawned with staggering clarity and she stared at him with wide eyes, her lips parted, trying to understand the unbelievable lightness of her heart suddenly. It was the first time she ever remembered seeing Alex look embarrassed, but even though he obviously didn't want to discuss it, she simply had to hear it confirmed. 'Alex, you haven't paid them yourself?'

He hooked a heel in the bottom rail of the fence and stared across the paddock with his brows drawn. 'It's to be a properly drawn up document, signed and sealed, to be sure there're no comebacks,' he promised, severely practical. 'I—we couldn't have you sued for defamation of character. Although that's frankly funny, when you think about it in connection with Blane McKinnon!' He spread his tanned arms along the fence rail and narrowed his eyes against the sun. 'Anyway, it's all settled now and we'll hear no more of it.'

Carla felt very humble and her eyes swam mistily as she looked at him. 'I—I don't know what to say, Alex. I——'

'Then don't say anything,' he advised shortly. 'I simply wanted to stop the rot before it went too far. I just—acted automatically, so don't let's make too much of it, huh?'

'Like you did when you pulled Tom out of the fire?' she suggested softly, and once more he frowned, as if he disliked having to admit to it.

But he turned and looked at her only briefly, then turned back to gaze once more across the paddock. 'Your boy-friend's been doing a gey lot of talking lately, hasn't he?' he remarked.

Moved by an irresistible need to be in touch with him, Carla ran a light fingertip along his arm. She felt the tanned skin flinch in response, but he kept his face determinedly averted and she noted long thick lashes making shadows on his ruggedly angular cheeks, and the way his thick, reddish-brown Hepburn hair curled a little just over his ears. A strong but occasionally very gentle man, who had been an important part of her life ever since she could remember, even though she had seen so little of him.

'You're a very much—*nicer* person than you let people see, Alex Hepburn,' she whispered, and for a moment curved her fingers over his arm, pressing into the firm brown flesh until he turned his head once more.

The brown eyes gazed at her for a second, warm and glowing and setting the wild excitement stirring in her breast again. 'Or mebbe I'm just a hot-headed Hepburn!' he suggested.

Impulsively she reached up her face and, standing on tip-toe, kissed his mouth. 'Thank you, Alex. For handling the McKinnons for me and for rescuing Tom.'

Briefly his eyes narrowed when she mentioned Tom, then he returned once more to his study of the paddock and the young animals at the far end who stood eyeing them with keen-eyed anticipation. His lack of response reminded Carla that it was Caroline Millar who now had first claim to his kisses; if Colin and Caroline herself were to be believed. And she felt a bitterness she would once never have thought herself capable of.

'If I'd known what a damned fool he was,' Alex told her harshly, 'I'd have left him to roast!'

Of course he didn't mean it seriously, but just the same his harshness made her shiver, as it always did, and she eyed him unhappily from the shadow of her lashes. Turning suddenly, he hitched up his denims and tucked in his shirt, obviously intending to bring the conversation to a close, but just for a moment his eyes held hers. Then they swept down slowly over every soft curve that her thin cotton dress showed off, and he laughed shortly.

'He's the devil's own luck, that man,' he said. 'I wish you joy of him, hein!'

'Alex!' He was already turned and walking away from her when she called him, and she noticed too that Caroline Millar was already putting in her daily appearance. Her car was drawing up in front of the house and she waved a hand at Alex as she switched off the engine. Her arrival, coinciding as it did with Alex's decision to leave, aroused all Carla's fighting spirit and her eyes blazed like green fire when she looked at him. 'I wish you joy of your Caroline too,' she told him, huskily angry. 'Did you forget that *she* knew about the McKinnons as well?'

She didn't wait to see what reaction she got, but turned quickly, and practically ran the length of the paddock, stopping only when she reached that tranquil section of no-man's-land between the two properties. Heaven knew why she had parted from Alex in anger yet again, but she vowed to herself that she would from now on remain at Hepburn's Quay, no matter if it did mean sleeping in the old house by herself. She couldn't come into such close proximity with Alex without betraying herself—and not for anything would she let him know how she felt, and give him cause to pity her.

CHAPTER NINE

It was simply because she did not want to arouse
Annie's curiosity that Carla spent the night at Hepburn's Carse after all. To have suddenly departed from
the now customary routine would have caused comment, and Carla was not inclined to explain her
reasons to the old lady. But Annie was far too shrewd
and observant not to notice that something was amiss,
and when the time came for Carla to return to her own
house, as she did each day just after breakfast, Annie
kept her talking.

'You've a face on ye as long as a fiddle,' she observed,
and patted the stool beside her with an insistent hand.
'Now what ails you, hein?'

'Nothing, Annie.'

'Och, don't lie to me, girl,' Annie admonished her
sternly. 'I ken well enough when a lassie is no as bright
as she ought to be, and there's a guid reason for a
moony look the like o' yours. Is it your man that's
troubling you?'

'Tom?'

'Is there any other man ye're mooning after?' She
was picked up quickly and sharply, narrowed dark eyes
watching her as she shook her head.

'No, of course not!'

'Of course nothing!' Annie declared. 'A girl as bonny
as you can set half the countryside on its heels wi' a
flick o' her brow if she's a mind to, and still hanker
after the one who disna come running with the rest.'

'Well, that isn't the case with me, I promise you!'

Carla shifted uneasily on the stool, trying to avoid

that shrewd and distinctly curious gaze. But Annie was as stubborn as a mule when she put her mind to anything; her husband had often been heard to remark that the Hepburns could teach her nothing about pigheadedness, though in this case it was kindly meant, Carla knew.

'Tom's getting along very well,' she went on, and sat with her hands clasped together around her knees while she talked. 'He shouldn't be long before he's out and about again now.'

'And yourself away with him?' Annie wondered.

'No.'

She left it at that, but Annie was not easily deterred. 'So there's to be no wedding, then?' she said, and did not bother to keep the satisfaction out of her voice when she said it. 'Alex tells me that it was he set the byre alight,' she went on, and ignored Carla's half-formed protest entirely. 'He'll have a gey lot of awkward questions to answer, surely. You're well out of it, child.'

'He'll need friends to stand by him,' Carla told her, and for a moment met the shrewd gaze steadily. 'I shall do everything I can to make things easier for him, Annie; Tom's been a very good friend to me.'

'Ooh aye, to be sure,' Annie agreed, and patted her hands consolingly. 'But he's no the man for you, ye ken that well enough now, d'ye not?'

'I suppose so, yes.'

'Och, it was plain enough for anyone to see,' Annie informed her. 'You'd have had no need to haver as you did about marrying him if you'd loved him.'

'You're very knowledgeable!' Carla smiled ruefully, then glanced quickly across at the door.

Footsteps tapped across the hall, brisk and business-like, and for a moment Carla almost held her breath, expecting Caroline Millar to put in her customary appearance. When whoever it was continued on past the sitting-room door she heaved an almost audible sigh of relief and relaxed once more on her stool. Caroline Millar was the last person she wanted to see at this moment.

But it was disconcerting just how observant Annie was for one of her years, and she regarded her for a moment with a raised brow and a hint of a smile on her round face. 'Caroline Millar'll not be coming here this morning,' she said quietly, and catching Carla's eye, challenged her to deny the assumption. 'You thought it was herself, did you not?'

'I—I thought it might be,' Carla admitted. 'You said yourself that she comes every day, Annie.'

'Not any more,' Annie assured her, and made no secret of the satisfaction it gave her.

Carla glanced at her curiously, and wondered at the sudden more clamorous beat of her heart. 'Did they have a row?' she ventured, and Annie laughed shortly.

'Ooh aye, they had a row,' she agreed. 'Though there was no mistaking who got the better of it eventually. Alex is a hard man when he sees a wrong done, especially to one he's fond of, ye ken. Yon woman is no used to plain speaking, and she did not take kindly to being called a mischief-maker, but then she should have had more sense than to let Rob Muir think it was you calling him about the McKinnons. Alex was mad too because he'd believed it of ye—the daft limmer!' she added disgustedly. 'He should have known ye better than that, and I told him so!'

Carla pleated the hem of her dress, absently watching her own restless fingers rather than look at Annie. 'Alex was so sure it was me and not Caroline, that was what made me so wild with him. That was why I made up my mind I wouldn't stay here last night, only'—she looked up for a second and met Annie's eyes uncer-

tainly, 'I didn't want you to be upset and wonder why I
was changing the routine.'

The old lady reached out and stroked her head with
thin, bent fingers. 'You thought Alex had spoken to her
about it?' she guessed, and once again Carla looked up
quickly and frowned.

'Why—yes. Didn't he?'

Shaking her head, Annie smiled. 'No, hein, you did.'

'*I* did?'

'You spoke to Caroline when you were in Gibbert,
did you not? In the coffee-shop, she told Alex.' Carla
nodded. The light was already beginning to dawn and
with it a sickening sense of her own fallibility. 'She told
him she'd no idea the McKinnons were involved until
you told her,' Annie went on. 'Is it not the truth,
Carla?'

'But I thought she already knew,' Carla protested.
'When she spoke about me having no special love for
the McKinnons because of the trouble I'd had with
them lately—I thought she knew. I thought Alex had
taken her into his confidence, and——' She did not
add that it had come as a shock to her, the thought of
his confiding such personal and insubstantial suspicions
to another party. Glancing up, she pulled a rueful face.
'Oh, Annie, I have been a fool, haven't I?'

'Aye,' Annie agreed with disconcerting frankness.
'But it's no been a complete disaster, and the air's been
cleared where yon woman is concerned, thank God! At
least she'll no be coming around every day and making
her moon-eyes at Alex.'

'You—you don't like her?' Carla ventured, and
Annie confirmed it unhesitatingly.

'I never liked her, nor her father either,' she declared. 'They were aye a pack of self-seekers wi' more
money than guid sense, and I'm relieved I'll not have to
share my home with her.' She sighed, seemingly with

satisfaction, and leaned back in her chair, closing her eyes for a moment. 'Aye, well,' she murmured contentedly, 'it's all coming to rights slowly. I've not too long left to me now, I ken it well enough, and I'd like fine to see you all settled in your ain proper places before I go.'

The fact of her counting Carla among her own family was not unexpected, for the Hepburns had always been a close family. Tom would have called it clannishness, but to Carla it brought a sense of comfort to know that she was as important in Annie's scheme of things as any of her granddaughters.

'Alex said something the other day,' Carla ventured, 'about letting Colin go to veterinary college after all. But I wasn't sure if he meant it, or if he was just talking wildly—he was angry at the time.'

Angry enough, Carla recalled, to threaten to let Colin go his own way and get himself another family; heirs who would presumably be more ready to accept what he had worked so hard to build up for his only son. She had, she remembered, assumed he had Caroline Millar in mind, but that idea now seemed less likely—completely *un*likely, if Annie's version of their parting was to be believed.

'He meant it right enough,' Annie assured her. 'You must have worked a miracle if ye managed to change that stubborn mind of his, hein, for I never could prevail upon him, and neither could Colin. But then,' she added with a wicked leer, 'ye're much younger and prettier than I am, and he'd be more keen to please you.'

'Please *me*!' Carla had started to protest that Alex's change of mind had nothing to do with her influence. But then she recalled how he had made that arrangement with the McKinnons to prevent them taking action for slander against her, and she examined the pattern on her dress rather than look at Annie. 'Whatever his reason, I'm glad he changed his mind for Col's sake, and I know he won't regret it.'

'No,' Annie mused, 'I don't think he will.'

'Which reminds me, I haven't seen Colin this morning,' Carla said. 'Is he too excited to eat this morning?'

'He's out with his father.' The old lady spoke quietly but her dark eyes gleamed with satisfaction. 'They went off together an hour and a half since.'

Carla clasped her hands together tightly and she smiled with delight. She knew just how much it would mean to Alex, even though he had given in on Colin's future, and she could feel his happiness as her own. 'Oh, I'm so glad,' she whispered. 'For both their sakes!'

'Aye,' Annie agreed. 'Alex was to try out the new stallion and Col asked to go with him. I've never seen him enjoy a moment so much,' she added, and for a moment her strong voice was softened and quieted. Then she looked down at Carla, still perched on the stool beside her, and the meaning in her eyes was unmistakable. 'I've no doubt they'll be back by now,' she said, 'and Alex would like fine to show you the new stallion. Why d'ye not go and find him, hein, eh?'

It was such an obvious move, and Carla was quite unashamedly tempted by the idea. But Colin and his father had a lot of time to make up and she was, quite unexpectedly, nervous of seeing Alex again, so she shook her head, smoothing down her skirt as she got up off the stool.

'I don't think I'll poke my nose in at this point,' she said. 'They have a lot of making up to do, those two, and I've quite a few things to do at home. I can see the stallion later on, there's plenty of time.'

'Ooh aye,' Annie agreed as Carla bent to kiss her. 'There's plenty of time.'

*

Carla had been cutting the grass with a mower bor-
rowed from the Carse, and she had made a pile of cuttings just outside the gate, with some vague idea in
mind that it might be of some use to Alex for his
animals. There was now an incredibly big heap of it
when she broke for coffee, and she surveyed the results
of her morning's labours with a sense of satisfaction.

It was surprising how much larger the garden looked
now that the grass had been cut down and most of the
weeds pulled up, and she felt pride in the fact that she
had done it entirely on her own, for Tom had never
shown the slightest inclination to join her when he was
there. Not that it was a big garden, but it had always
looked so neat and tidy in her grandfather's day, and
she wanted to see it looking the same again, whether or
not she would be staying there herself.

She felt much more lighthearted since her talk with
Annie earlier that morning, and she attributed that as
much to the fact that Caroline Millar had been more
or less given her marching orders as to anything else.
Working outside suited her too, for she revelled in the
sunshine, and had already acquired a quite passable
tan. The light golden sheen on her skin and the warm
flush in her cheeks gave an added brightness to green
eyes, and she was smiling to herself as she made her
way around the house to check on a fire she had going,
burning up some of the weeds.

She had no idea she was no longer alone until Alex
spoke immediately behind her. 'Good morning, Carla.'

Turning swiftly, she stared at him for a moment
with wide startled eyes, her heart thudding hard; because he had startled her, her common sense insisted.
But the longer he continued to stand there the harder
it beat, and it was to ease the rather breathless silence
that she eventually laughed; a small unsteady sound.

'You startled me,' she accused. 'I didn't hear you come.'

Alex glanced down at his feet, set firmly apart on the grass-grown path. 'I'm wearing boots as I always do,' he pointed out.

She glanced across to where his mount was tethered to one of the fence posts that helped support the ragged hedge. The new stallion, she supposed; apparently he was as anxious to show it off as Annie had suggested. Glancing around the garden, he noted the tidier borders and the mown grass.

'I see you've been busy,' he said. 'But why didn't you ask for some assistance, Carla, it's too much for you to tackle on your own.'

Turning right around to face him, she brushed a forearm across her brow and blew through pursed lips at a persistent strand of hair that still clung there. She was warm, and the violent beat of her heart added to the flush in her cheeks as she stood there, much too disturbed by the gaze of those steady brown eyes.

'I—I just didn't think of it,' she confessed.

'Or you wouldn't ask me for help,' Alex suggested, and she tilted her chin at the hint of challenge.

'Feminine pride,' Carla told him, and he laughed.

'Sheer pig-headedness,' he insisted. As if he anticipated an argument and sought to avoid one, he placed an arm around her shoulders and drew her towards him, looking down at her with that same disturbing steadiness. 'You didn't wait by the paddock this morning,' he told her, 'so I had to come and find you.' He was taking her with him, along the pathway towards the gate. 'I want to know what you think of Saladin.'

Since the animal had moved around where she could see him through the broken-down gateway, she took note of the new acquisition while they walked. It was as tall as the indomitable Grey had been, but more slen-

derly built, and it was a glossy golden brown with an
arched neck and a long silky mane. He was much more
handsome than Grey had been and she could understand how proud Alex must be of it.

'He's a beauty,' she approved. 'He looks as if he's got
some Arab blood, has he?'

'Pure Arab,' Alex proclaimed with obvious pride.
'He cost me a gey lot o' siller, as Grandmother says, but
I think he'll prove worth every penny of it.'

His arm around her shoulders brought her into close
contact with him, and made little thrills of pleasure
flutter along her spine. But his words reminded her of
something else too, and she cast a swift, searching
glance at his face before she mentioned it. 'I wish you
hadn't made that arrangement to pay the McKinnons,'
she said. 'It must be an added strain when you've paid
out so much for the stallion, Alex.'

The arm about her shoulders slipped down to en-
circle her waist, tightening its hold until hard fingers
pressed deep into her flesh, and she caught her breath
at the increasing flurry of her pulse. 'It's done now,
hein,' he told her, 'and there's no need to feel badly
about it. I suppose I should have done something for
them over the years, as McKinnon says.'

'*Why* should you?' Carla demanded. 'You don't owe
them anything! You even found them a better cottage
to live in so that they didn't have to move into the
town. They have no cause for complaint!'

Alex looked down at her flushed face and the angry
glow in her green eyes and he smiled and shook his
head. 'You're a wee battleaxe when you're roused,
aren't you?' he asked softly. 'But you don't have to get
so het up over it, Carla, it's over and done with now,
they'll not mention that business again. Once Col's
away at college he'll not be seeing them very much, and
until he goes he'll be having to keep his head down and

study if he's to get the passes he needs. I think they'll mebbe miss him.'

He would think of that, of course, Carla realised. It was one of the numerous things she had discovered about him in these past weeks; the fact that he was capable of such compassion and understanding. She hadn't noticed it nor even looked for it, in her hero-worshipping days, and she wondered yet again how she could have been so unaware of the real man behind the ruggedly virile autocrat she had adored.

They were there by the gate with the object of admiring his new acquisition, but for the moment the handsome stallion was virtually ignored, while Alex stood beside the untidy and overgrown hedge with her. She kept her eyes downcast while she spoke, and she was startled to hear the breathless unsteadiness of her own voice.

'There was a bit of a muddle over the McKinnon business,' she said. 'I—really I suppose it was my fault in a way, because I told Caroline Millar what we suspected, thinking she already knew about it.'

'You thought I'd told her, so Grandmother tells me?'

She glanced up, nodding reluctantly. 'It was the way she spoke; I mean, I thought you'd told her because—Oh, Alex, I didn't realise and I should have done, I suppose, that you wouldn't have told anyone else about it.'

'Which was why I thought you were Rob Muir's little stool-pigeon,' he teased softly. 'I didn't see who else it could be.'

'I'll pay you back,' Carla insisted. 'Whatever you've arranged to have paid to the McKinnons, you paid because you thought I was responsible and I'm very grateful for that. But I'll pay you back, I promise. You can—we can take it off the price of Hepburn's Quay.'

'Ooh aye?'

His manner made her unsure suddenly, and she looked up at him and frowned, her eyes anxious. 'Alex, you do still want the Quay, don't you?' When he did not immediately answer, she moistened her lips anxiously, not sure what to think. 'Alex?'

He stood facing her and with his hands resting heavily on her shoulders, his brown eyes dark and unfathomable. 'Well now,' he said, apparently having given it some thought, 'if it means you going back to London with yon man——'

'I'm not going back to London with Tom, I *told* you! I'm not going anywhere with him.' She glanced up at him and just for a moment her green eyes gleamed with mischief and speculation. 'He says he's going to lure Caroline away from you.'

'Is he now?' He seemed only mildly interested in Tom's plans to rob him of his erstwhile girl-friend, but his eyes were fixed on her mouth and seemed to be watching every word she formed with an intensity she found increasingly disturbing. 'He can have Caroline, as long as he leaves you here—*I* don't want her. I never did, for all you kept trying to marry me off to her.' He slid his hands down to her upper arms and held her lightly, his eyes all the time on the soft uncertainty of her mouth. 'I want *you*, hein!'

'Alex——'

She gave a cry of alarm suddenly when he stepped closer and in doing so unbalanced her so that she tumbled backwards into the pile of grass cuttings beside the gate, taking him with her. Though he could almost certainly have saved himself if he had but tried.

Shaken for a moment and breathless with the wild pounding beat of her heart, Carla looked up at him; at the darkly tanned face and deep brown eyes. He was pressed close, almost on top of her and with his hands again on her shoulders, keeping her buried deep in the pile of fresh-smelling grass that tickled her skin and worked its way into her dishevelled hair.

It was warm and soft and as comfortable as a thick feather bed, and she had not the slightest desire to move at the moment. She was dazedly aware of experiencing a whole gamut of new emotions, all of them pleasurable, and of a wild, exultant kind of excitement that persuaded her to follow wherever Alex led.

Then he inched himself nearer, until the lean weight of his body pressed her even deeper into the grass. His face hovered above her, a face that was for a second strangely unfamiliar in its expression. 'Will you stop havering, woman?' he demanded in a voice so much more fierce than the look in his eyes that she felt her whole body shiver in response. 'Either marry me, or keep your damned house and find yourself another buyer!'

Carla stared up at him, her lips parted and her heavy-lidded eyes dazed and questioning. She had not expected that; though she could not have said what exactly she did expect at the moment. Marrying Alex was something she had always dreamed of when she was a romantically-minded teenager; it seemed too much to accept that it was actually coming true.

Alex, never the most patient of men, took advantage of her silence to add persuasion to his demand, and leaning further over her, he sought her mouth, gently at first but with a breathtaking hint of passion that stirred her to respond. She closed her eyes, her lips parted, appealing and submissive, yet as passionate as he was after those first few seconds.

It was like a burning hunger in her, she realised as she clung to him; an almost unbearable ecstasy that seared through her whole body and consumed her. His mouth and the strong, gentle persuasion of his hands brought her into a new world, a thrilling and demanding world that was everything she had always dreamed of, and more. Alex, as a lover, fulfilled every promise she had always expected of him, ever since those days when she first began to see him as a man, and not simply as a grown-up, distant cousin.

When he raised his head at last she found herself looking directly into the brown eyes, so close and so alive with desire that she drew a deep shuddering breath. 'Well?' he demanded, and she moistened her tingling lips with the tip of her tongue before she replied.

'You really want to marry me?'

'Of course I do, ye daft wee limmer!' he declared forcefully, and once more impressed his determination upon her mouth. 'Am I not asking you to marry me? And I warn you, I'll not take no for an answer! God knows I've loved you for long enough, and you'll surely not deny you love me, for I know better!'

Challenged by his dogmatic confidence, Carla turned her head quickly from side to side. 'Oh, you're so sure I'll say yes, aren't you? It hasn't even occurred to you that I——'

'It occurs to me that you're havering, woman,' he told her sternly, and holding her face between his hands he looked directly into her eyes. 'I'm a Hepburn,' he reminded her. 'Old Johnnie would not have wasted time arguing with a woman who wouldn't make up her mind—you know it!'

'And you mean to follow in his footsteps, do you?' Carla challenged. Her eyes were bright and gleaming and she was aware with every nerve in her body of the lean, virile length of him, half burying her in the soft and sweet-smelling grass. 'A wicked old rapscallion, who——'

Alex's mouth silenced her very effectively, and she reached up after a second or two, to put her hands behind his head, grasping his thick reddish-brown hair in her fingers to bring him even closer. On the other side of the gateway the big stallion tossed his head and whinnied impatiently.

'Wheesht,' Alex told him, briefly turning his head. 'Wait, you impatient brute!'

Snuggled deeply into the drying grass, Carla smiled up at him, her hands clasped behind his head. 'Maybe he thinks he's waited long enough,' she murmured, and laughed softly when Alex turned back to her, his brown eyes dark and glowing.

'So have I,' he said, again seeking her mouth. 'So have I, my love!'

JOY
ROMANCE
LOVE

Harlequin Omnibus

THREE love stories in ONE beautiful volume

The joys of being in love...
the wonder of romance...
the happiness that true love brings...

Now yours in the HARLEQUIN OMNIBUS
edition every month wherever
paperbacks are sold.